Misplacing Paradise

Puzzling Through Romance Series

Miranda Herald

My Koala Pouch

Contents

Also By Miranda Herald

Loves Cats Series:

Prequel Chapters: Willa's Blooper Reel

FREE at www.mirandaherald.com

Book 1: Loves Cats, Anonymous

Book 2: Swipe Right for More Cats

Book 3: Free Shipping with More Cats

Puzzling through Romance Series:

Prequel Novella: Blundering through Paradise

FREE at www.mirandaherald.com

Book 1: Outwitting Paradise

Book 2: Misplacing Paradise

Book 3: Hiding Paradise

Smitten Scientists

Book 1: Catch and Release

Book 2: The Turtle and the Hare

Book 3: Wild Goose Chase

Chapter 1
All Dressed in... Flames

Brianna

“The bride is on fire!”

Brianna stopped walking down the aisle, mortified.

I'm the bride!

The guest nearest to her jumped up from their chair, causing it to go flying backwards into the guest behind. Chaos erupted on the beach around her, and Brianna smelled smoke. Panicking, she started running back down the aisle, trying to get the flames as far away from the guests as possible.

Should I stop, drop, and roll in the sand... in my wedding dress?

She was a few feet away from the ceremony but veered toward the ocean.

“Brianna!” She heard her name being yelled as someone grabbed the veil off her head, sending bobby pins flying. She spun around, eyes searching wildly to see Nathan, her future husband. He threw the veil onto the sandy ground and stomped on it until all the flames were out.

Brianna looked around at her dress and saw no other signs of fire. Nathan bent down, picked up the blackened lacy white veil, and held it out. He watched her carefully, as if waiting to see if she would laugh or cry. A crowd was gathering around them, her mother the first among them. Nathan gave Brianna a small smile and whispered so only she could hear, “You ran away from our wedding.”

Taking a deep breath, Brianna looked up at him and gave a soft chuckle before smiling shakily. "What can I say? When I saw who I was about to marry, I decided to swim for it!"

They laughed together, and Nathan pulled her into a hug and rested his chin on the top of her head. Soon, Brianna felt small arms wrap around her legs and heard the high-pitched voice of her soon-to-be step-daughter, Jenna. "I'm glad you're okay. Do you want me to get you a bucket of water to keep you safe while you marry my daddy?"

Brianna patted Jenna on the shoulder as a photographer snapped photos of the future family holding the burned veil. "I think I'll be all right now, honey. I'm just going to give those tiki torches a bit more space."

Nathan moved her to the side and checked her over. "Would you like to try again or reschedule?"

Brianna looked around at the crowd murmuring amongst themselves and gave them a smile to let everyone know she was unharmed and feeling fine. She hugged Jenna to her side and looked back at Nathan. "I know we pulled this wedding together quickly, but I can't wait to marry you, Nathan. Let's try again. I didn't let any of the puzzles and traps on your island deter me. I'm not about to let a little thing like being a blazing bride impede our happy family."

Nathan turned to the crowd. "If everyone could make their way back to their seats, we are going to try to get married again."

The crowd moved in a very unorganized fashion. Brianna's mother blew her a kiss. "Good luck, honey!" She heard faceless voices from the crowd say, "Someone keep an eye on the aisle. That girl can run!" and "Blow out all the torches or she'll catch her hair on fire next." She hadn't been nervous before, but now her stomach was filled with butterflies.

Nathan headed back to a small platform that overlooked the sea and stood beside the pastor. Brianna led Jenna back to the beginning of the aisle. She eyed the tiki torches that were stuck in the sand and lined the edges of the aisle. Small wisps of smoke trailed out of the tops where someone had extinguished them.

Take two of getting married. Hopefully, this time, she wouldn't have to run away. *Just watch. I'll probably trip and fall on my face during this go around.* She was lucky that a handsome, wealthy man like Nathan wanted to marry her, but how many times would he have the patience to try again?

Brianna's best friend, Mavis, came back with them and messed with Brianna's long brown hair while the violin trio played again. She whispered in Brianna's ear, "Just keep your eyes on the rich guy in the suit and you will be fine."

After rolling her eyes, Brianna smoothed her dress out and tried to calm her nerves. She looked down the aisle to see her good-looking groom, Nathan, standing there with his dark hair slightly mussed from running his hand through it, and his cummerbund made the pooch around his middle stand out slightly. He stood with a wide grin, patiently waiting for her. It was all she could wish for.

Jenna looked up at her, and her short brown hair, all curled and pinned to the top of her head, hardly moved. With wide, doe-like eyes, she whispered, "I'm all out of flowers."

Taking a handful of flowers out of her own bouquet, Brianna quickly took the petals off and dropped them into the little girl's basket. With a big smile and a quick hug, Jenna started down the aisle. Happily, the six-year-old girl sang *Happy Birthday* while walking down the aisle. It melted her heart, and Brianna heard the guests muttering, "Aw."

Looking around, Brianna saw the breathtaking beauty of her paradise island wedding. Everything was perfect. The sun shone brightly, but not too hot. The turquoise ocean was smooth, with small waves lapping the beach. Her mother and best friend came out for the occasion, and best of all, she was no longer on fire.

The music changed to the *Wedding March*, and Brianna walked down the aisle toward her bright future where she would live happily ever after. Luckily, she didn't believe in superstitions or bad luck at weddings. Her life was now going to be like a dream come true.

The ceremony was short but beautiful. The reception was full of delicious food, dancing, and laughter. After things were winding down, Brianna sat on the cool, slightly quieter edge of the party, watching her guests drink and dance the night away. Today had been fun, yet exhausting. She'd met so many new people from Nathan's family and work that her head spun.

Tomorrow, they would visit with family and friends and say their goodbyes. After spending so much time planning the wedding, she hadn't had time to pack for the honeymoon. She would have a few whirlwind days to pack up their belongings for the next three months. They were taking Jenna and going to Scotland to follow the treasure map Brianna found on this very island. She was so excited; she couldn't believe she had to wait days to leave.

Before long, Nathan found her and joined her on the outskirts of the party. He softly murmured, "If you want, we can sneak away. My brother offered to put Jenna to bed for us tonight."

Looking at him out of the corner of her eye, Brianna smiled. It felt like a long road to get here. She fake yawned and stretched her arms. "Yeah, I am getting mighty tired. I'm sure I will fall asleep as soon as my head hits the pillow."

Leaning down, Nathan gave her a slow kiss that made every nerve in her body fire. She kissed him back eagerly, gripping his strong biceps, letting her lips do more of the talking than her words.

Brianna heard someone clear their throat, causing her to break her focus on her new husband and look up. She didn't recognize the man, but there were so many business associates and friends that she had barely met.

"Excuse me. I hate to interrupt, but I thought you would want to know that your daughter got sick all over the dance floor. She's asking for you two."

Nathan ran his hand through his hair, and Brianna gave him a small smile. "I'm sorry. I think someone had too much cake when she knew I was otherwise occupied watching you."

Brianna pulled his arm as they started heading toward the dance floor hand-in-hand. "It's okay. If Jenna needs us, then we'll be there. There will be time for us later." The adoption paperwork was all filled out and ready to be sent in tomorrow morning. Soon, Jenna would be her daughter too.

With so many people blocking their way, Nathan moved to the right, and Brianna moved to the left. They looked at each other and chuckled, as neither of them could make progress before letting go of each other's hands and making their own way to find Jenna.

Chapter 2

Late for Her Honeymoon

Brianna

Five days later, Brianna walked out of the bathroom and into the new bedroom she shared with her husband. *I'm late for my honeymoon*, she thought as she looked at a clock on the wall. Nathan would be waiting to take her away from paradise, and she didn't want to delay him any further. She shouldn't have taken such a long shower, but the hot water felt so good waking her up.

After grabbing a Pop-Tart from the kitchen, she rushed through the lush jungle as the sun rose, cautiously watching her feet to avoid any snares and traps. The last thing she needed after the chaos of packing up to leave for three months was to be stuck in a net hanging six feet in the air... again.

She speed-walked toward a small cottage near the beach, and a large dog burst out from under the porch, tongue hanging out to greet her. A small monkey on Brianna's shoulder climbed onto her head as it scolded the dog. "Hello, Suzie. It's nice to see you too. Make sure to be nice to Chee Chee for me, okay?"

After patting the dog, she moved toward the cottage, carefully avoiding the hidden sink traps, and knocked on the door. Nathan's head of security, a large man with dirty blond hair and a short beard, answered, and she heard puppies barking and whining in the background.

"Hello, Dugan. I'm just here to drop off Chee Chee. Thank you so much for taking care of him while we're gone." After giving the monkey a little pat, she handed him over to Dugan.

The monkey chattered but settled down on Dugan's shoulder. She was going to really miss the little guy. He was her almost constant companion, and her shoulder already felt empty without him. Dugan smiled and patted the monkey. "Don't worry, ma'am. I'll take care of this little guy like a penguin with its chick. Everything will be fine, and he'll be waiting for you guys to come back. Have fun. You deserve it."

Tapping her foot, Brianna was eager to keep moving, but instead, she pulled an envelope out of her pocket and handed it to him. "This is from Nathan. He wanted to drop it off himself, but we just ran out of time this morning. Thank you for always going above and beyond, Dugan. I don't know what we would do without you."

Dugan shrugged and opened the envelope. A hand-drawn card from Jenna featured Suzie on the front. Inside was a nice-sized bonus check. "Tell him thank you, but I'm happy to do it. Last night, I personally packed all the bags you left for me on the plane to make sure nothing got mishandled. I hope you guys find some treasure!"

Brianna took off from Dugan's cottage and jogged toward Otter's Cove, where the boat was picking them up. She rushed past beautiful bird of paradise flowers and vibrant green ferns. Colorful birds called out from the treetops as monkeys swung through the trees. She would really miss her home on Riley's Paradise Island, but it would only be for a few months. She was sure their honeymoon would feel like it was over too quickly, and everything would be here when they returned.

Brianna tripped on a root and fell on her hands and knees on the dirt path that Dugan carefully kept cleared for them. She wiped dirt off her pants, but it left stains and didn't come completely clean. Frowning, she let out a loud sigh. She had picked this outfit out specifically because it was both cute and comfortable. It was her favorite, but at least she didn't ruin the top. *Oh, well. Nathan probably wouldn't recognize me if my klutzy self showed up perfectly clean, anyway.*

She jogged past the little treehouse without a ladder. She chuckled to herself, remembering how confused she'd been trying to figure out the riddle to get up into the treehouse and then how exasperated she felt when she realized it was all just a gigantic trap. Almost a year ago, she'd met Nathan for the first time at that very spot.

Last night, she and Nathan agreed to split the last-minute things they needed to do in the morning. They'd set an alarm for five a.m. He was going to get Jenna fed and ready, and Brianna was supposed to drop off Chee Chee. After their charges were cared for, the three of them would meet at the boat that would take them to the plane that would take them to Scotland.

They had a private boat and a private plane, so she knew they wouldn't leave without her, but being stressed and running late really wasn't how she wanted to start their honeymoon. She and Nathan were only married a few days ago, but it seemed like they kept finding silly little things to fight over. The last thing she wanted to do was make him late.

She started jogging down the path again and ran straight into a man with dark shoulder-length hair and a goatee. Nathan's brother, Jackson.

Will I ever make it off this paradise island?

He grabbed her arm as she struggled to keep her balance. "Brianna! I'm so sorry. I was hoping to run into you guys before you took off, but not literally."

Brianna was pleased she didn't land on her behind again, but she stepped back and tried to straighten out her new outfit. "You almost missed us. We were supposed to be gone, but it looks like I'm holding up the boat. I hope we don't put the plane too far behind schedule too."

Jackson walked at a comfortable pace toward the docks, forcing Brianna to slow down and join him. "Oh, you worry too much. Now that you're a Riley, you realize that people build in extra time. They expect rich people to be late."

Frowning, Brianna looked at him from the side of her eye. "I don't think things work like that. No one likes to be late."

Shrugging, Jackson handed her a gift bag. "Ah, it is what it is. Here, I brought this for you guys. I know Nathan prefers playing with those video games he makes, but if you get bored on the long plane ride, I thought you might want to beta test the new game I made. It's called 'Escape from Dr. Jekyll.' If all goes well, Dad would like to add it to Riley's Games' launch roster in a few months."

Picking up her pace, Brianna tried to get Jackson to walk faster, but he refused to be rushed. "Thank you. That was very thoughtful. We will check it out, but I don't know how much free time we will have on the plane. We still have a lot of that treasure map to figure out and, so far, those riddles are stumping us."

Brianna spotted the ocean not too far ahead when something hurtled toward her legs, making her arms fly out to keep her balance. Jenna looked up at her with large, bright eyes. "We've been waiting for you forever! I'm ready to go to a castle and find real pirate treasure!"

Hugging the little girl, Brianna took her hand as they walked the rest of the way to the beach. "I ran into a few things along the way, but I'm here now. Let's get going." Standing by the shore, smiling, was the kind, handsome man she agreed to adventure through life with. Nathan.

He seemed unperturbed by her tardiness. That was good. They really had a lot they still needed to learn about one another. She gave him a quick kiss and smiled at the man Nathan had hired to pick up supplies and make island deliveries. It was one of the many changes they were making, to increase the security and paid help on the island.

"Wasn't it a team of two guys you hired?" Brianna asked Nathan.

He nodded. "Yeah. The other guy just went inland because he said he drank too much water on the…"

They heard the man yelling, and Nathan took off running toward the jungle as Brianna stayed at the docks and held Jenna. Only a few moments later, both men re-emerged, laughing. Nathan patted the man on the back. "Sorry. I probably should have warned you." He turned to Brianna. "He just got caught in one of the slip-knot traps we have scattered around the island. Now that more people are going to be wandering around, I guess I'll have to have Dugan clean some of them up."

After they got engaged, he'd made a bunch of plans, and she wasn't sure exactly what things would be like when he was done. Brianna raised her eyebrows to ask how he was feeling with all of the new-comers because he was quite suspicious when she first met him. Before she could say anything, Nathan continued. "Maybe it will be good for Jenna to live with a small community, but don't worry, there will still be plenty of puzzles and traps around. I don't think I would feel totally safe without them, and I don't want to risk Riley's Paradise Island losing its charm."

While Brianna was excited about going on their trip, she felt a bit of sadness about all the changes. She agreed they needed more help, with the amount of maintenance this place required, but she had a foreboding that things would never be the same. Last year, she uncovered the beauty and mastered the quirks of this island, all the while falling in love with the man of her dreams. What would this next year bring?

Chapter 3

Plane Debacle

Brianna

Brianna looked at her new husband in shock as dark soda dripped down her face and onto her shirt. It was completely ruined. Nathan's chiseled features looked on with wide eyes, and his jaw dropped. After the initial surprise wore off, he hurriedly snapped into action and scooped up a handful of napkins to hand her. "Here, let's clean you up."

Nathan winced as she quickly grabbed the napkins from him, and he ran his hand through his wavy dark brown hair. "I'm so sorry! Turbulence made my glass go flying. Don't worry, we will get you fixed up and into something fresh to wear. Dugan would have stowed all of our bags in the back when he packed the plane for us."

Brianna cleaned herself up as well as she could, but there wasn't much she could do about her soaked chest. She brushed out her long, sandy-brown hair with her fingers and glanced down at her slightly plump hips, all dry. At least it didn't hit her hair. A shirt was easy enough to change.

She glanced over to check on Nathan's daughter. *No, not only Nathan's daughter.* They were still waiting on some paperwork to go through, but she needed to get used to thinking that Jenna was now going to be her daughter too. The little girl was so engrossed in a game on her tablet where she cut up fruit that she didn't even look up during the spilled drink incident.

After taking a job as Jenna's governess last year, Brianna felt very close to her, but it would still take some time to get used to thinking of her as her daughter. *A daughter... that would make me a mother. I really hope I don't screw this up.*

Sighing, she turned to the man who had asked her to marry him only a few months ago. Nathan was a handsome man who always dressed to impress. *He never seems to get himself messy like I do.* "Where can I find our bags?" she asked him.

Nathan led her to a room at the back of the private jet. Dugan had neatly secured all of their bags so that none of the luggage could move. Nathan looked around. "What did your bags look like? I see mine and Jenna's, but not yours."

Brianna gave the room a thorough search but didn't find any of her bags of clothing or toiletries. Even the box containing the glass-making supplies she used to make detailed animal figurines was nowhere in sight.

"Where else would Dugan have put my bags? He would rather shoot himself in the foot than disappoint you. For the head of security on your island, he does a lot for you that is out of that wheelhouse. I think you should start calling him your butler."

Nathan frowned. "I think Dugan would rather shoot himself in the foot than be called my butler. I know he does a lot. That's why we started interviews to get him some more help around the island. There really is nowhere else that we store luggage on the plane. Are you sure you left it in the entryway like I told you? Beside the big plant?"

Her mind's eye pictured her clothing hundreds of miles away on Riley's Paradise Island. "The entryway near the big plant? That's the one we use every day. I put all of my things in the main entryway to the house with the blue tile. Are you telling me that everything I packed to go away for three months is just sitting in a pile back at home?"

Her things were in Nathan's hacienda-style home, in the middle of the jungle, on the mostly deserted island full of puzzles and traps. She wrung her hands together, and her anxiety grew as she mentally ticked off everything left behind. No clothing. No hairbrush, and no deodorant.

Nathan winced. "Yep. It looks that way. I'll let you borrow one of my shirts, and we can have Dugan ship everything to the castle. We can buy you anything you need for a few days until it comes. You should be more careful about putting things in the right spot next time." Nathan rummaged through one of his bags and pulled out an oversized collared white dress shirt and handed it to her.

Brianna's cheeks turned red as her temper rose at his last comment. She loved the man passionately, but it seemed like, since they were married, they were having a lot of trouble transitioning from an employee-and-boss relationship to one united in holy matrimony.

Hopefully, this time away from their normal routines would help them find a better balance in their relationship. "I put my bags where you told me. You said to put them in the entryway, and I put them in the entryway. *You* need to be clearer in your communication."

Nathan smiled at her mischievously. She frowned back at him, but apparently, he was trying to defuse the situation. "I wouldn't mind if you decided to just forgo clothing altogether for the next few days. This is our honeymoon, after all."

Brianna rolled her eyes. "Way to change the subject when the heat is on you. While this is our honeymoon, you forget that your six-year-old daughter is on this adventure with us as well."

Nathan retreated out of the room. "You get changed. I'm going to get out the copy we made of the treasure map. We will be in Scotland in only a few hours, and we need to come up with a plan for deciphering these clues and determining where we want to look first."

All anger forgotten, the thought of the treasure map made Brianna's heart flutter in excitement. She had found it by accident while exploring Riley's Paradise Island. While they could decipher some of the map she'd found, it still held many mysteries.

After a few weeks of scouring maps, they eventually figured out that the map was of a remote area in Scotland around Dunam Castle. They were on their way there now.

Brianna smiled to herself. *The hunt for treasure is on!*

After walking to the bathroom, Brianna wiped the rest of the sticky residue off of herself and changed her shirt. The large white dress shirt hung past her hips so loosely that she took off her belt and secured it around her waist over the outside of the shirt. She looked at herself in the mirror before leaving. *I look like a gentleman pirate. All I need is a tricorn hat.*

Brianna went out into the main part of the plane that was modeled after a living room. Nathan had a copy of the map spread over the table and a mirroring map of the local area around their destination, Dunam Castle. It was a close-up map of the nearby town of Tober, only twenty square miles, in a rural part of Scotland.

Nathan wrote a few notes in a small leather journal, while studiously examining one of the riddles. At first, he didn't seem to notice her re-entry into the room. The location of the map had not been easy to identify. They had scoured maps for weeks until they found a match. After digging a little deeper, they were shocked to find out that Nathan's elderly estranged aunt had recently purchased that very castle because she believed it was connected to their family. To their delight, she was renovating the place and seemed happy to have them stay for the summer.

The familial connection made Nathan all the more determined to find the treasure the map led to. He believed his great-grandfather who settled the island must have left it for his descendants for a reason. Brianna suspected that Nathan was just as excited to learn more about the original owner of this map as he was the treasure itself.

Moving closer, Brianna looked over Nathan's shoulder. He looked up at her and smiled. "You always look so sexy when you wear my clothing. I think I should hide your clothes on purpose."

Feeling better now that she knew she would have her possessions soon, she playfully swatted his shoulder. "Then I'll steal yours. I'm sure you would just love having to wear my clothes several sizes too small!"

Holding up his hands in surrender, he said, "All right, you win!"

Suddenly, his smile transformed into a grimace. "All playing aside, I just talked with the pilot. There are some pretty severe storms near the airport we were planning on landing at. We found another private airport a few hours' drive north that should work for us. We will just have to rent a car and travel to the castle from there."

Nodding her head, she gave him a half smile. "Thanks for the update."

Brianna studied the map for what seemed like the hundredth time. She could match up the topography similarities between the two maps but was very unsure beyond that. The treasure map was full of weird riddles and five small drawings of mystical-looking creatures.

There was a sea serpent, a wolf-faced man, a dragon with no wings, a naked woman with hooves, and even a small, dirty man dressed in rags with a broom. Nathan had the riddles translated from Gaelic into English, but they still made about as much sense as they had when in a foreign language. They hoped that once they were physically in the map's location, they would have better luck.

Brianna finally broke the silence. "I think we should get a feel for the area and maybe show these symbols to some locals. Maybe they could direct us to what they mean or where they came from."

Nathan shook his head. She swore he never seemed to like an idea unless it was his own. "No. I think we should systematically check out the big landmarks in the area. Especially the areas closest to the symbols. We can cross them off this copy of the map and look around for clues."

The plane shook again, the turbulence getting worse. Jenna ran over to Nathan and flung her arms around his waist. "It's okay, Little Bird. The turbulence is just from the storms that we're flying through. We will land soon."

Jenna looked at the map, feeling better, but unwilling to leave her father's side. She spoke up excitedly. "Do you really think we'll find the treasure? I think there will be gold coins, and gems, and a diamond princess crown. I bet a dragon will guard it."

Nathan laughed as he hugged his daughter close. "If there is a dragon, we will fight him off. Don't worry, Little Bird. I will keep you safe. If there is a diamond princess crown in the treasure, I believe it would fit perfectly upon your head."

Jenna turned to Brianna. "What do you think the treasure will be?"

Brianna thought for a few moments. "You know we might not find the treasure at all, right? Or someone else could have already found it."

Jenna looked at Brianna and gave a heavy sigh, as if exasperated by her lack of imagination. "I know that, but what if we *did* find the treasure?"

Brianna smiled. She was thinking of the chocolate coins she had ordered that looked like real gold pieces. Even if they didn't find genuine treasure, she thought Jenna would be excited to "find" a yummy treasure near the end of their trip.

Brianna responded, "I would love to find a sword to fight that dragon with you. Maybe we will also find a chest full of doubloons."

Brianna squinted one eye and held up a pretend sword. She approached Jenna, knelt in front of her, and made her best pirate impression. "Arr, matey. If ye landlubbers be takin' me booty, I'll have to take me revenge." Then Brianna tickled Jenna, who squealed with laughter.

Forgetting about the turbulence, Jenna went back to her tablet game. Brianna looked at the map from where she knelt. From this angle, the weird symbols stood out on the map, but she couldn't see the topography very well. If she connected the dots like a constellation, it kind of looked like a person. *That makes no sense. If I bring it up to Nathan, he will just brush off my thoughts like he has been doing a lot lately. I'm sure it's nothing.*

Chapter 4

Slinging Mud

Brianna

After staring at the map for a few hours and bickering with Nathan over the meaning of one of the riddles, Brianna needed a break. Jenna was napping, so she went to the back room of the private jet and called her best friend, Mavis.

Mavis answered on the second ring. "Are you in Scotland yet? Is it beautiful? Do you have a cool accent yet?"

Brianna chuckled. "Not quite. We're still on the plane. I just needed a break from staring at that map... and from Nathan."

Mavis responded with so much sass that Brianna could picture her with a hand on her hip and the other hand waving through the air. "What did he do? If I need to fly out to Scotland and slap him, I will. Just say the word."

Chuckling, Brianna was feeling better already. "No, I'm fine. It's just been hard. I guess after I married a sweet, handsome, rich guy on a paradise island, I figured I would live happily ever after. Ugh, I know I'm just being whiny. I have so much going for me, and I wouldn't change anything. I just feel like Nathan sometimes still treats me like his employee. I give a thought or want to do something, and he just bulldozes over me and does whatever he wants. You don't even have to tell me. I know I should talk to him about it, but everything is so new. I don't want to be a pain. Thanks for helping me get that off my chest. How are you doing?"

After pausing a moment, Mavis jumped in. "I'm sorry you're going through that, but rest assured, you're never a pain. I'm sure it's going to be a tough transition for you guys. As for me, I broke up with my boyfriend, hate my job, and my best friend moved to a weird, quirky island. At least when we lived in the same apartment, we could eat ice cream and be miserable together."

Forgetting about her own problems, Brianna's brow furrowed in concern for her friend. "Aww. I'm so sorry, Mavis. I know you said things weren't going great with your boyfriend and your job, but I didn't realize they had gotten that bad. Have you started applying for new jobs? Babies are being born every day. I'm sure there are lots of places that need midwives, and you're always welcome to come and visit me in Scotland this summer."

A bit more upbeat, Mavis quickly replied, "Yes, I have applied, but I haven't gotten a job offer yet. You know, I think I will come and visit you. I haven't seen you since you decided to be a candle on your wedding day. That will give me something to look forward to. Why don't you give me a call when you get settled and we can set something up?"

Brianna gave a sigh of relief. "It will be great to see you. I need my best friend around more often."

"Perfect, then we will make it happen. I need to get back to work, but you let Nathan know that if he isn't good, we might just need to go hunting for some sexy Highlanders. Eh, even if he is good, maybe I'll go hunting for one myself!"

Brianna hung up with Mavis, feeling calmer. Sometimes it felt good to be heard and reconnect with someone who wasn't Nathan. She sure missed her best friend and could already picture trying to hold her back as she chased after every eligible Scotsman that showed off a bit of chest hair. It would be good to see her.

Before long, the plane landed. Her first impression of the country was of pouring rain and foreboding gray skies. Hopefully, the castle they had rented from Nathan's aunt for the summer would be more welcoming.

The three of them rushed from the plane into a small rental car. They took a few of their essentials with them, but the rest of their bags would be following. In her bag, Brianna had a map to help them get to the castle, but it started at the airport they were supposed to land at, not the one they did land at. She tried to use the GPS on her phone, but the storm was making an error pop up. They started driving, and Jenna fell asleep almost immediately.

It was raining so hard that they could barely see the road. Brianna was looking at the map and tried to direct Nathan, who was driving. "You should turn down that road. It says seven miles to Tober, where our castle is located."

"No, if we follow the shoreline, that will eventually lead us right to the castle we're staying at. The castle is only a few miles from a bluff overlooking the sea."

Brianna felt more and more uneasy as the rain continued to pour and they got into more of a rural area. The sunset and the lack of natural light made the roads even harder to navigate. Soon, they were only driving on dirt roads.

Brianna said, "Maybe we should just stop for the night. We passed a bed-and-breakfast a few miles back. We could be back there in twenty minutes and find the castle tomorrow. In the daylight."

Nathan growled, obviously frustrated by the strain of driving under such harsh conditions. "I don't want to drive backwards twenty minutes when we could keep driving forwards and be there in a half hour. I just want to get settled into our new home for the summer."

Suddenly, their car slid off into a ditch where the water had washed out the road. Nathan groaned and laid his head back against his seat. He tried to back the car out and then tried to go forward, but the car's wheels just spun in the mud. Amazingly, an exhausted Jenna slept through it all.

Nathan turned to Brianna and took out his frustration on her. "Don't distract me when I'm trying to drive! It's raining hard out there. Here, you stay in the car with Jenna. I see a light up ahead. I'll go get us some help."

"Well, if this is all my fault, then I'll take care of it. *You* stay in the car, and I'll go get help. I need some space from the ego filling this car anyway." Brianna opened the door, darted out into the pouring rain, and disappeared into the night. Nathan watched her go with his brow crinkled in concern. "Brianna, please come back!" Heedless of his words, she sped walked away. He sat there helplessly, unable to leave Jenna and follow.

Chapter 5

Muddy in a Pub

Brianna

Brianna stomped down the road. The rain soaked her to the bone in moments. It wasn't long before she stopped caring about the mud and rain and splashed in the biggest puddles on purpose. She may have been wet, cold, and muddy, but at least Nathan didn't get to tell her what to do.

Some honeymoon. She loved the man, but she wasn't expecting how hard things would be. It felt like they were both trying to navigate this new dynamic from employee and employer to married couple, and lately, all they were doing was fighting.

Now that she had put a bit of distance between them, she felt better. Maybe she was just a little stubborn, but they were alike in that way. Both Nathan and she always wanted to get their way. She couldn't help smirking. She was shivering, but it was somewhat worth it to see his exasperated look as she hopped out of the car.

Brianna looked in front of her at the light in the distance. It was farther than she had thought from the car. She could cut across the field she was walking beside and decrease her walk significantly. She was getting frozen. *I really hope that light leads to warmth.* Looking down at herself, she groaned. She had forgotten that she was still wearing Nathan's white dress shirt belted around her waist. *I'm soaking wet, dressed like a pirate, and have nothing to change into when we reach the castle we're staying at for the summer. Ugh.* Day one of their honeymoon was not going well, and she hoped that her forgotten bags would make it to them soon. On the bright side, any residue from that sticky soda Nathan spilled on her had washed off in the rain.

Brianna climbed over a split-rail fence. She looked around the pasture through the rain and saw nothing in sight. Whatever lived in the field was smarter than she was and had found somewhere to stay dry. Brianna hastily made her way across the field, always heading toward the light. She finally felt like she was making progress. Walking quickly, Brianna came upon a large stone structure in the middle of the field. Should she give it a wide berth or use it to get a break from the rain? She was studying the building so hard that she stopped paying attention to where she was placing her feet.

One foot stepped directly into a large cow patty. Before Brianna knew what was happening, she went sliding face-first into the mud. *I really hope that is only mud!* She lay there a few moments, letting the rain pour down over her. *Could I be any more miserable?*

Suddenly, Brianna felt hot breath on the back of her neck. She got the feeling of something looming over her. She turned her head and saw a large reddish-brown nose inches from her face. She scrambled backwards, trying to get out of the way of this beast. *What have I gotten myself into now?* Brianna looked up, up, and up, seeing the massive body of a cow. It had long hair that covered its eyes and two very large and pointy horns. Mud and water covered the animal as it moved its nose closer to investigate who was trespassing in its field. *God, please don't let me get eaten... alone... in this field.*

"I'm sorry! I'm leaving right now. Please don't eat me!" Brianna yelled at the cow. The cow sniffed her again and then retreated under the open rock shelter where she noticed a dozen more shaggy, bedraggled cattle.

Brianna got to her feet and walked backwards, away from the cattle. After she made it a few yards away, she started running toward the light. She slipped in the mud and fell but got up and kept going.

Through the rain, she could hazily make out a large building not far ahead. She climbed the split rails of the fence faster than she thought possible. She bent over, panting, and looked back through the rain. In the darkness, she could see no sign of anything moving nearby.

Brianna took a deep breath and walked the last few yards to a small building with a floodlight on the top. She made it across another dirt road when she noticed a sign hanging on the front of the building. A large snakelike dragon curled around the words, Beihir's Pub. It looked a little like a serpent Brianna had seen on their treasure map.

She opened the door and took a step inside to see one small room with a bar on one side and about a dozen tables on the other. The pub's walls, trim, and furniture was constructed of old, dark wood with tables and chairs that appeared sturdy but well-used. It was small and didn't look like it had had any paint jobs or renovations in decades. The focal point of the room was a mural of the same dragon-like beihir spread across the back of the bar. Its claws extended as if grabbing a bottle of alcohol lined up on the shelves below it.

Upon seeing Brianna, the handful of occupants went silent. They stared at her, and more than a few jaws dropped. A few couples were sitting at small tables in the middle of the pub. One pair unabashedly stared, their relation to one another unmistakable, with matching cleft chins. Another couple eyed her nervously but didn't let it stop them from finishing their meal. There was a handful of men drinking around a bar. One thin man looked at her in disgust, while another younger but more burly man looked curious.

A beautiful brown-haired waitress swayed her hips from side to side as she walked up to Brianna in a skimpy outfit. Her cleavage was hanging out, and her skirt was so short that one wrong move would show off her underwear, or lack thereof. She left very little to the imagination.

Hand on her hip, she chewed on a wad of gum and looked at Brianna skeptically. None too kindly, she remarked in a nasal voice, "Look what the cat dragged in. What are you doing here, hun?"

Brianna looked down at herself, covered in mud and pieces of grass. She noticed the puddle that was forming on the floor where she dripped. Brianna desperately wished she had thought about bringing her purse. At least then she could have bought a hot drink or left a good tip for the mess she was making.

Brianna wondered if everyone would have been more friendly if she was clean and had her six-year-old step-daughter with her. That little girl could make friends with anyone. Then again, Brianna was a stranded woman in obvious distress, and no one seemed to care. Maybe she was just staying in a grumpy area of Scotland.

Frozen by all the unforgiving stares, Brianna replied with the first thing that popped into her head. "I'm here on my honeymoon."

Brianna tried not to wince as the beautiful woman gave out a grating laugh, in total contrast to her looks. "Looks like you lost your groom, hun. From the smell of you, I would guess you lost him in the pasture. Or did you take a liking to our Scottish Highland cattle?"

Chapter 6

Lost Groom

Brianna

Brianna, miserable and humiliated, sharply retorted, "I need to contact a tow truck driver. Our car is stuck up the road in the mud. We need help to get out… and directions to Dunam Castle."

The woman's nasal voice grated on Brianna's nerves as she responded, "So, your new hubby sent you out in the rain to get help, did he? Great start to a marriage. Let me get you Hector's number. He has a truck that can help you, and he lives in a little cottage near Dunam Castle. Although, why you would want to go to that old, haunted dump, I couldn't guess. You wouldn't be foolish in looking for that fabled treasure, would you?"

"It's really none of your business, but we aren't just aimlessly looking for a fable. I found a treasure map," Brianna said stiffly.

The woman was blessedly silent as her eyes grew wide. She muttered under her breath, "Well, I'll be," and headed off.

After the woman left, a large, stocky man with dark hair and a matching beard got up from the bar and walked over to Brianna. He was the one who was looking at her curiously when she came in. She eyed him warily. *He sure is handsome, but his stature kind of reminds me of the Scottish Highland cattle I recently met.*

He carried a jacket and offered it to Brianna. "I couldn't help overhearing. Welcome to Tober. Don't mind Florine. We don't get many strangers around here that don't know her ways."

Brianna smiled at him. The strong brogue accent differed from what she was used to hearing, but that seemed about to change. *Maybe I'll pick up a bit of an accent by the end of the summer, just like Mavis suggested. Wouldn't that be charming?* Brianna took the coat but hesitated to put it on. "Thank you, sir, for the coat, but I can't take it. I'll get it all muddy."

The man offered his hand for Brianna to shake. "My name's Lewis. I live a few miles from here. Believe me, it has seen more than enough mud in its days. Get yourself warm. This is a small community. If you're staying at Dunam Castle, I'm sure we will run into each other again. What should I call you? What brings you to these parts?"

Brianna put the warm coat on and hugged it to herself, trying to warm up. "My name is Brianna. My husband and I are staying at Dunam Castle for our honeymoon. We found an old map and intend on trying to figure out where it leads us."

Florine walked up with a scrap of paper with a phone number on it. She looked Brianna up and down critically. "Let's hope you find a new pair of shoes in the treasure at the end of your map. Those aren't salvageable for anything but growing flowers in." She handed Brianna the paper. "Anyway, I called Hector. He will be at your car in about twenty minutes to help you guys out of the mud. Here's his number if you need to get a hold of him again."

Florine looked down at the puddle that continued to grow around Brianna's feet. "If you wouldn't mind waiting in your car, I'll send him out when he gets here." Florine walked away to bus a table, having obviously dismissed Brianna.

Brianna looked hungrily at the nearby diners' meals. *I would give anything for a turkey sandwich right now.*

Lewis nodded his head toward Brianna. "Well, it was nice to meet you, Brianna. If you and your husband want some fresh eyes on that map of yours, let me know. I've lived in these parts my whole life and might be a bit of help."

Brianna smiled gratefully at Lewis. "Yes, we will definitely take you up on that. We aren't even sure where to start looking! Thank you so much for letting me borrow your coat."

Brianna turned, stiffened her spine, and took a deep breath before walking back out into the pouring rain. This time, Brianna stayed on the road and walked around the long way instead of cutting through the pasture. She saw the headlights of a few vehicles pass through the intersection ahead of her, but none made their way up to the long road to the pub. Her borrowed coat soaked through swiftly, but at least she felt a little warmer than before.

Brianna could finally see their rented car in the distance and realized the tow truck had already arrived. She walked up to the truck to see Nathan and a bright-eyed Jenna sitting in the back. A large older man in a bright yellow raincoat was hooking the car up to the truck. Brianna went back to introduce herself. At this point, she had stopped caring about being in the rain. A few more minutes wouldn't make a difference.

Brianna called out to catch the man's attention. "Hello. My name's Brianna. Are you Hector? Thank you so much for coming out in the rain to help us!"

Hector turned toward her. He was a large man with an even larger beer belly. Beyond that, it was hard to see any of his features between the rain, darkness, and his hood. Hector reached out his hand to shake Brianna's. "Nice to meet you. Florine called, so I was happy to help. I met your husband, Nathan, a few minutes ago. He was pretty worried about you when I beat you here."

Hector went over to his tow truck and pushed a button so the chain linking the truck to the car started to reel in. With a lurch, the car moved out onto the road. "I hear you three are on your way to Dunam Castle. Happens that I live nearby and keep up with the grounds for the castle. Once I get you safely on the road, you can follow me there if you want."

Brianna nodded. "That's very kind of you. Thank you. We would appreciate the help. After the day we've had, we're exhausted and can't wait to fall into clean, soft beds. That is after I get a nice hot shower."

Hector looked over at Brianna. "Do you want a bit of advice?" Brianna nodded. "Beware the brownies." Brianna stood there, confused, as Hector went back to work. Maybe the man was crazy. *Was he referring to my weight? Should I beware the chocolate chip cookies too?* Sure, she could afford to lose a few pounds, but she'd never had someone be so straightforward about it.

Hector got their rental vehicle centered on the road and then went to his tow truck and opened the door. He yelled to Nathan, "She's all ready for you."

Nathan bundled Jenna up and rushed her back into the car. Mid-dash, he saw Brianna. He got Jenna settled in the back seat and turned to Brianna. Relief was clear on his face as he ignored the rain. "Brianna, I was so worried! You were gone for such a long time, and then the tow truck driver got here before you. Thank goodness you're all right."

Brianna smiled at him, glad he cared. "Come on, silly. Get in the car. You at least aren't soaking wet yet."

Nathan ran around and jumped into the driver's seat while Brianna took off the coat she had borrowed. She placed it on the seat of the car before sitting down. It was wet, but at least it wasn't covered in mud and goodness knows what else from her jaunt through the pasture.

Nathan looked over at her quizzically. "Where did you get that coat?"

Brianna was more concerned about the hot bath and soft bed she was daydreaming of. She pointed ahead to Hector's truck that was pulling away. "Don't let that truck out of sight. He said we could follow him to Dunam Castle."

Nathan scowled slightly and followed Hector. "You know I could have gotten us there myself, right?"

Brianna patted his arm, too exhausted to even think about arguing again. "I know you could have gotten us there, but this is a good way to start a relationship with our new neighbor for the summer."

Mollified, Nathan followed Hector for about twenty-five minutes. Hector stopped his truck and waited in the opening of a driveway to a small cottage. Nathan had just enough room to pull up beside Hector's truck and stay on the road. The two of them rolled down their windows.

Hector yelled through the window, "This is me. Keep going straight. You will see the castle ahead in just a few minutes. Florine said she gave you my phone number. Let me know if you need anything."

Nathan nodded. "Thanks, Hector. I appreciate all of your help tonight. I won't forget it." Then he raised his window and drove on down the road. After a few minutes, the outlines of a castle appeared in the distance.

Excited butterflies danced in Brianna's stomach. *Maybe Nathan did this kind of thing regularly, but growing up, I was lucky if we took a vacation every few years. I can't believe we're staying in an actual castle.*

A refreshed Jenna hopped up and down in the back seat. "Are we there? Is that it? It looks so spooky! I bet it's full of ghosts!" Jenna seemed to contemplate that for a moment and then added in a quiet voice, "Can I sleep in your room tonight?"

Nathan answered, "Don't worry. There is no such thing as ghosts. As for sleeping arrangements, we'll see when we get there, okay, Little Bird?"

They drove up to the courtyard of the castle but had to park farther away because of a downed tree. They exited the car and ran to a stone archway that led to the castle's courtyard and front entrance.

Boulders from the stone surrounding wall had fallen into the courtyard. A part of the roof was missing from one of the spires. A turret leaned awkwardly and looked dangerously close to falling off.

The castle was in ruins.

Chapter 7

Castle of Ruins

Nathan

Nathan glanced at Brianna out of the corner of his eye. He didn't want her to know that he had been anxiously watching her face for disappointment and frustration since the disastrous previous evening. She was dressed in another one of his shirts and knelt down, helping Jenna unpack her bags.

This was not how he had pictured his honeymoon to go with his new blushing bride. This castle was not the romantic getaway he had imagined. They found that the men his aunt hired had remodeled the main interior of the castle, including their bedrooms and the kitchen, but the place still looked like a work-in-progress at best and ruins at worst.

The right and left wings had caution tape over them, and some parts of the structure looked like they were ready to fall right off the castle. *I will have to keep a close eye on Jenna so she doesn't go wandering around by herself where it isn't safe.*

He made the reservation for this place through his aunt, Priscilla Riley. While they weren't particularly close, he had trusted the older woman when she described it as a "newly remodeled charming castle close to a majestic bluff." The place had sounded perfect. He had tried calling her several times since arriving, but she wasn't answering her phone.

Jenna came over to him, full of concern, and sniffled. "I've left Theodore behind! He must be so lonely!"

Nathan gave her a reassuring hug. "It's all right, sweetheart. We can have Dugan ship Theodore over with Brianna's things. I'm sure Dugan is taking good care of him while we're away, just like he's taking care of Chee Chee."

Jenna ran back and helped to place her clothing into her drawers. Brianna laughed as Jenna acted out the dragon she was convinced was guarding the treasure. *I'm so lucky those two get along so well.*

Brianna was a strong woman. One thing he loved about her was her ability to keep going through all obstacles. It sometimes seemed as if she could do anything when that stubborn streak of hers activated. He loved her with all of his heart and didn't want to provide a life for Brianna that she had to persevere through. How could he tell if she was really doing all right?

He had hoped this trip would be perfect. He'd imagined this treasure hunt being an exciting adventure that would bring all three of them together as a family. Unfortunately, all they did was keep bickering over the most mundane things. Maybe this trip wasn't such a good idea after all. They could have left Jenna at home with his father and gone to the Bahamas for their honeymoon like a normal couple.

Brianna teased Jenna, "You know, when I was at the pub last night, it was called Beihir's Pub. There was a picture of a large, wingless, serpent-like creature. It kind of looked like the one that is guarding the sea on our treasure map. Maybe a dragon is guarding the treasure!"

Jenna squealed gleefully. "I will start working on armor for us right away! We will also need shields..." Jenna got an art kit with markers and paper out of her bag and drew all of the supplies she could think of for dragon fighting.

Since Jenna was occupied, he decided to try to make some relation-ship headway with his wife. "Brianna? Do you mind if we talk?"

Brianna nodded and followed him out into the hallway. There were six remodeled bedrooms on this floor. Two of them had private bathrooms installed, the other four shared a bathroom that opened to the hallway. They headed toward the largest master bedroom.

"Brianna..." Now that Nathan had her alone, he didn't know what to say. He ran his hand through his hair as he started again. "I'm sorry this trip has started so poorly." Nathan stopped in the hallway and looked at her with lips pursed and brow furrowed. "I'll make it up to you, I promise."

Brianna stared up into his eyes. "I know you try. We both do. I've been thinking about it, and I think we're having a hard time transi-tioning. I was your employee, and now I'm your wife. You were used to being independent and making all the decisions for yourself and Jenna. Now I'm here, and I want a say in our life too." Brianna started to tear up as she added, "Maybe we got married too fast. It just felt so right at the time."

Nathan froze as he heard her last words. *She can't be saying what I think she is, can she?* He flashed back to the wedding a few weeks earlier. Brianna had looked so beautiful walking up the beach in her wedding dress. He had felt like the luckiest man in the world. Well, at least until she caught fire.

Everything had gone splendidly. It had thrilled Jenna to be a flower girl. Brianna's mom had flown in for the occasion. His father had been on his best behavior, but then again, he'd asked Debbie to go with him. She wasn't acting like a housekeeper as much anymore, but at least she could keep the old man in line. He was such a hypocrite when he gave him a hard time about dating his employee, and now he was making a move on his.

Brianna broke off his thoughts. "Well, what do you think?"

Nathan looked into her eyes and gave her a quick kiss. He was so busy reminiscing that he had forgotten exactly what she had asked him. He played it safe. "I love you. We will work all of this out. It just takes time."

The two of them heard the knocker pounding on the front door. Nathan said, "You stay here and finish unpacking. I'll see who it is. Maybe it's my aunt apologizing for renting us this wreck of a castle and she has come to give us a refund."

Nathan opened the door, and a warm breeze washed over him. Very different from the cold stone and musty-smelling upstairs. He would have to see if a few windows would open up there. The birds were singing, and he imagined he could see the weeds in the courtyard growing. It looked like the area was thriving after the previous day's storm.

A woman with brown hair, dressed in a tight-fitting dress, was standing in the entryway. She seemed a bit surprised when Nathan opened the door. She held out a basket toward him. In a nasal voice, she said, "Wow, aren't you handsome? My name is Florine. I met your new wife at the pub the other day and thought I would check in on her."

Nathan took the basket and peeked inside. There were chocolate brownies inside. *How thoughtful.* "Thank you so much, Florine. My name is Nathan. We are going to be your neighbors for the summer. Thank you for stopping by. I'll tell Brianna you came. I'm glad to see she's already making friends."

Nathan noticed the gardener, Hector, trimming some of the high grass across the courtyard. Nathan was going to call out to the man, but Jenna came running to the door. "Daddy! We have a visitor!" She thrust her hand into the basket and snatched a brownie before Nathan had a chance to react. "Yummy!"

Florine's eyes turned to saucers upon seeing the little girl, but she leaned over to speak to Jenna face to face. "Aren't you a cutie? Brianna didn't mention that you brought a cute little munchkin on your honeymoon with you!"

Jenna's mouth was still half full when she asked, "Why do you talk funny?"

Nathan intercepted before she said something impolite about the nasally quality to her voice. "Little Bird, the people here think you speak funny. We live in a different place, so we have different accents. We just aren't used to hearing people from Scotland speak."

Florine looked up at Nathan and batted her eyelids. "You know, I have a lot of babysitting experience. After my father came here from France and married my mother, they had me and my twelve little brothers and sisters, and I looked after them. You should let me watch her while you spend some time alone on your honeymoon with your new wife."

Nathan thought to himself for a few moments. Florine didn't dress like the best role model, but it was very nice of her to bring over a welcome gift. She had obviously made friends with Brianna last night at the pub, and he trusted Brianna's opinion. *I really need some time alone with Brianna to get my marriage back on track. Maybe this is the perfect opportunity falling right into my lap.*

Nathan warmly smiled as he reached out his hand for her to shake. "That is such a generous offer. We might take you up on it! Do you mind providing me with your full name and address to run a quick background check on you? It's my policy for all employees."

Cocking her head, Florine opened her eyes wide and batted her lashes. "If you really feel that's necessary, I'll give you all of my information because I have nothing to hide. You will see, my background is sparkling clean." She took a piece of paper and pen out of her purse, jotted down her name, and handed it over to Nathan.

Nathan glanced down at the paper in his hands. "I'm sure you're right. We need a bit of time to get oriented here, but we could set something up for next Friday? Would that work for you?"

Florine gave Nathan a wide smile. "Of course, I'll make the time for you two lovebirds. What are neighbors for?"

Florine left, and Nathan felt his phone buzz in his pocket. He had missed two calls. One was a message from Jackson. His voice was eager. He was obviously very jealous that he didn't get invited to come on their treasure hunt.

Jackson's message was brief. "Hey, Natey boy! I hope you aren't missing paradise too much. Have you found the treasure yet? Let me know if you get stuck and need some help." Nathan didn't bother calling him back.

Dugan, his head of security, didn't leave a message. Nathan gave him a quick call. "Hey, Dugan. I was just calling to see how everything is going. I was also wondering if you could send Brianna's luggage. We left it behind."

"Well, I'll be a worm on a sidewalk. I'm sure she must be very upset. I'll send it over right away. You can also tell her that Chee Chee misses her but is doing fine staying at my cottage. Although, the messy little critter keeps knocking things over and throwing things around."

Nathan smiled to himself, glad he had someone so dependable back at his home. He felt completely at ease leaving Riley's Paradise Island to the care of Dugan. "Thanks, Dugan. Oh, and if you could grab Jenna's bear, Theodore, and send it too, she would really appreciate it."

Nathan gave a sigh of relief that everything was good to go at home. He always felt better when he fixed things. His chest puffed up as he walked back up the stairs. Things would be fine now that he'd set up Florine to watch Jenna. Brianna would be so pleased to have a friend around, and it would give him more time to mend his relationship with Brianna. *I can't wait to tell her, but maybe it would make an even better surprise!*

Nathan was heading back upstairs when he heard a loud clatter coming from downstairs. He quickly changed directions and entered the newly remodeled kitchen where the loud sound seemed to originate from. A handful of glasses from an open cupboard were lying broken on the kitchen floor.

Chapter 8

Beware the Brownies

Brianna

What a beautiful day! Brianna stood still and let the sunshine soak into her skin. They'd had a nice day right after they got here, but the last few days had been rainy and overcast. Today was a real treat. She held a large basket with a light lunch inside. Now, they just needed to find the perfect place for a picnic.

Jenna ran excitedly around the courtyard. "Look! I caught a toad!" Jenna held up a wiggling brownish-green creature. She gave an anguished cry as it broke free and hopped under a bit of rubble. After several minutes of unsuccessfully trying to recapture him, Jenna ran off to explore again.

Nathan stepped up behind Brianna and wrapped his arms around her. "Today really is beautiful, isn't it? The perfect day to explore the castle grounds. Do you mind if we stop in and see Hector before we wander too far? With the shape this place is in, I want to hear exactly what his duties are at this castle. I still haven't been able to get a hold of my aunt. I think she's avoiding my calls."

Brianna smiled and closed her eyes, simply enjoying the feel of his embrace. Despite the slight hiccups in their relationship, there wasn't any other place in the world she felt more comfortable and safe. She didn't want to move. Without opening her eyes, Brianna responded, "Sure. I'm just happy to get out in the sunshine and not be cooped up in the castle another day and I'm so thankful my luggage arrived. I appreciate you getting it shipped here so quickly."

Nathan leaned down and kissed her on the forehead as Jenna called out, "Come look, quickly! Look what I found!" Jenna held something small up, but it was too far away for Nathan and Brianna to make out. They broke apart and moved toward Jenna.

"What is it, Little Bird?" Nathan inquired.

Jenna jumped up and down excitedly. "It's my favorite hair pretty! How do you think it got out here?"

Brianna took the clip and examined it. It wasn't wet from the rain. Could the sun have dried it already? "Maybe it fell out of your hair on the day we arrived. We rushed to the castle pretty quickly in the downpour. It wouldn't surprise me if we dropped something."

Jenna frowned and shook her head. "It can't be. I wasn't wearing it the first day we arrived. I was wearing it yesterday, and I didn't come out here yesterday."

Nathan shrugged but looked around with his eyes narrowed. "Let's just be thankful that you found it."

They made their way southwest down the road and walked about two miles before they saw the turnoff for a small cottage. Jenna alternated between running way ahead of them and stopping at every flower and weed until she fell way behind them. They walked up the driveway and knocked on the door.

Hector answered. "Hello! Nice to see you. I was just about to sit down for a bit of lunch. Would you care to join me?"

Nathan shook his head. "No, no. We don't want to disrupt your meal. We are out for a walk to explore the castle grounds and brought a picnic basket along. I just wanted to stop by and say hello. Thank you again so much for helping us with the car."

Hector seemed pleased by the appreciation. He tousled Jenna's hair, but the little girl ran and hid behind Nathan's legs. "Happy to help. I wouldn't have wanted this wee lass caught out in the storm."

Coming out from behind Nathan's legs, Jenna took the acknowledgment as an opportunity to add her two cents. "I just found my hair pretty!" She held it up and showed it off to Hector. "Although I don't know how it got outside. I didn't leave it out there."

Hector looked at her straight-faced and slightly nodded his head. "You know, lass, this is brownie country. Brownies are little critters that help you around the house doing chores and such. Although, they expect an offering to be left out at night, such as a saucer of milk. Otherwise, they are liable to cause lots of mischief."

Jenna's eyes grew wide. "Do they cause mischief like knocking glasses out of the kitchen cupboards and knocking a lamp over in my room?"

Hector nodded. "Could be. I choose to leave some milk outside of my door every night, just in case. Every morning, the bowl is empty."

Nathan changed the subject before Hector could tell Jenna any more nonsense. "So, Hector, you mentioned you take care of the castle grounds. I was just curious. Do you work for Priscilla Riley who owns this castle? Do you have a way of getting hold of her?"

Hector nodded his head. "Yes, I do work for Ms. Riley. Last year, she bought Dunam Castle in total ruins. She hired an entire crew of men to fix up the main part of the castle. Then she got sick and had to put the project on hold. She asked me to keep up with the weeds and keep the local wildlife out until she was better enough to oversee construction again."

Hector went inside, grabbed a piece of paper, and wrote a phone number on it. "She called me a week or two ago to let me know she rented the house out for the summer. She said she wasn't feeling well enough to be here and welcome you herself, so she asked that I keep an eye out for you. Here's her phone number."

Nathan took the piece of paper and looked down at the number. "That's the number I couldn't reach her on. Thanks anyway. Do you have any recommendations for a good picnic location?"

Hector smiled. "There is a stream that lies straight west of Dunam Castle that's nicely shaded by the trees. Not only is it a great fishing spot, but a pretty little spot too." Hector's eyes sparkled as he looked at Jenna and added, "Lass, if you are really quiet, you might even spot a kelpie sunning herself on a rock. Just don't get too close."

Nathan turned away from the door when Hector interrupted with a last question. "What brought you out this way? We don't normally see many strangers around here. They mostly stay closer to Loch Hernessy."

Jenna piped in, "We found a treasure map! We're here to find dragon-guarded pirate treasure!"

Hector's eyebrows rose. "Well, I'll be. Best of luck to you." He gave Jenna a wink, then turned back to his cottage, tapping his head as if deep in thought.

Chapter 9

Kelpie Spotting

Brianna

On their walk, Jenna's feet hurt, so Nathan hoisted her up on his shoulders. They made it back to the castle's courtyard and were already getting hungry and tired. Brianna didn't feel like they had made much headway in their explorations. She wasn't ready to go back inside and be cooped up in that big, cold castle, so she cheerily tried to add extra pep to her voice. "Only a little farther for our picnic!"

They could see a tree line not too far in the distance, so they continued. As soon as they entered the forest, the temperature felt a few degrees cooler. It was a welcome relief from the sun that was quickly reaching boiling temperatures. As soon as they could hear a trickle of water, Jenna shushed them anytime one of them said anything.

Soon, they came to a moderately sized stream. They could see large sea trout swimming along. There was a splash. Jenna looked at Brianna wide-eyed. "Do you think that was a kelpie?"

Brianna laughed. "Jenna, honey. Brownies and kelpies are pretend things that people like to use their imaginations to believe are real. A kelpie is a black horse that walks on water and turns into a human with hooves. Does that sound real to you?"

Jenna dropped her head and shook it slowly. "No, I guess not."

Brianna gratefully sat down and took a blanket out of the basket she was carrying. Nathan laid the blanket out along the bank, and the trio hungrily ate the turkey sandwiches she had packed. After their stomachs were satiated, Brianna dug through her basket, confused. "Well, that's funny. I could have sworn I packed a few apple fritters for dessert." Brianna looked suspiciously at Nathan and Jenna. "Did either of you two eat them?"

Nathan and Jenna innocently shook their heads. Nathan stood up. "Well, now that we've eaten and rested, we had best start our way back."

Jenna lay on the blanket dramatically. "My legs hurt. I couldn't possibly walk another step. I'll stay here and keep a lookout for kelpies, just in case."

Nathan lifted Jenna onto his shoulders as Brianna finished cleaning up the rest of their picnic area. They headed back through a small patch of forest before entering the hot, grassy area that stretched a few acres around each side of the castle.

The sun beat down on Brianna, and all she could think about was how nice a cold cup of lemonade would taste in the cool stone castle. She was ready to go back now. A shower would be refreshing too.

"What do you think about the castle grounds?" Brianna asked Nathan.

Nathan looked around the fields. "Well, that definitely was a beautiful spot by the stream, although Hector sure seems to be superstitious. I'm not sure if he really believes all the old Scottish folklore or if he was just putting on a show for Jenna."

Brianna replied, "Either way, it doesn't really matter. We're only here for the summer."

Nathan cut off the end of Brianna's statement. "I don't care how long we will be here. It irks me that he's putting hocus pocus into my daughter's mind. I don't know what it is about that man, but I don't trust him."

Brianna looked over at Nathan with one eyebrow raised. "What's wrong? Hector has only been kind and helpful to us. He has done nothing to deserve your dislike. If he's upsetting you with his superstitions, talk to him and kindly ask he not say anything like that around Jenna."

Sweat pouring from her brow, she and Nathan bickered back and forth the rest of their walk back to the cabin. Some people thought old bickering couples were cute, but Brianna was realizing it was just plain exhausting. No matter what either of them said, it seemed to escalate their disagreements. She really needed some space.

"You need to be more sensitive to other people's cultural beliefs."

"Hector needs to mind his own business."

"He was minding his own business until you went to his cottage!"

"You're supposed to be on my side!"

To Brianna's relief, when they got back to the castle, they saw an unfamiliar truck parked in front of the courtyard. It looked like they had company, and she really didn't want to argue in front of other people. In order to stop their argument in its tracks, Brianna purposefully ignored Nathan. She made no outward rude behavior toward him but needed some time to cool off before she talked or even looked at him.

Lewis stepped out from behind the truck. Brianna lit up at seeing the man who had shown her such kindness at the pub. She cheerfully shouted ahead of her. "Lewis! Welcome! Thanks for stopping over. I have your coat all cleaned up and ready for you inside. It will just take me a few moments to grab it."

Without turning toward Nathan, Brianna monologued her shared history with Lewis. "Lewis was a kind stranger that helped me at the pub. He even let me borrow his jacket when I was soaking wet in the rain."

Nathan quietly grumbled, "You wouldn't have needed to borrow his jacket if you had stayed in the car like I asked."

When they got closer to Lewis, Brianna made introductions. "Would you like to come in and have some lemonade with us while I fetch your coat?"

Lewis shrugged. "Sure, I could do that. I'm also here to offer my services, looking at that map of yours." He turned to Nathan. "When your beautiful wife told me about your treasure hunt, I offered to look for you fine folk. I have lived here all my life and might recognize something that you wouldn't. Where did you find the map, anyway?"

Before Nathan could answer, Brianna jumped in. "Yes, that would be lovely. Thank you so much for offering to help us! I found it hidden in a cave back home at Riley's Paradise Island." Nathan ground his teeth but said nothing.

Lewis stroked his beard. "Hmmm. You know, Captain Angus Kiddle the privateer grew up around these parts in the 1600s. In his later years, he traveled pretty far. I wonder if you have a map of his hidden treasure. There are fables it's hidden around here, but I've explored this entire area. It may have many secrets, but a hidden treasure isn't one that I have found."

They all walked inside, and Brianna led them to a drawing room that held a table with the map laid out. Brianna pointed. "Here's the map. I'll let you take a peek while I get lemonade and your jacket. Jenna, why don't you come with me to help with refreshments?"

Jenna helped for a few minutes and then grew bored and ran off to her room, trying to spot a brownie. Brianna was gone about ten minutes before she came back to the drawing room, arms full.

Brianna dropped the jacket and lemonade in her hands, the jacket turning into a wet sticky mess at her feet. Nathan had drawn one of the swords on the wall and stood poised to attack. At the other end of the blade, stood a defenseless Lewis.

Chapter 10

Wulver Hunting

Brianna

Lewis picked up his lemonade-covered jacket off the floor. He held it out from his body and looked back and forth between Nathan and Brianna. "Why don't I take this home before it has any more mishaps?"

Nathan and Brianna stood glaring at one another and didn't answer him, so Lewis walked past them both. "I'll just let myself out. I've told Nathan all that I could think of for the moment, but there are a few puzzling things I'm going to think about. Let me know if you need any more help with the map."

Lewis brushed past Brianna on his way out, and Nathan lowered the sword and hung it back on the wall. As soon as Lewis was out of earshot, Brianna yelled at Nathan, "What is going on? Were you going to skewer our guest right here? What if your daughter had walked in?"

Nathan returned the outrage. "What were you doing making gushy eyes at this stranger? Did you forget your new husband was right behind you?"

Brianna was too angry to think rationally. She narrowed her eyes. "At least he treats me with respect instead of just bossing me around all the time."

Nathan clenched his jaw shut in a steely silence that was worse than if he had yelled at her. She decided she wouldn't be the first to talk. They stared at each other, unblinking, and a long silence ensued as their argument turned into a battle of wills. *I feel like I'm in elementary school having a staring contest.*

Nathan broke first. He gave her a small half-smile. "Were you really only worried that I would stab him in front of Jenna? You wouldn't have minded if she was nowhere around?"

Brianna took a deep breath, and her features softened. "You may have grown up like a barbarian out on that island, but no stabbing people. Ever."

Having defused the bomb in their conversation, Nathan's half-smile turned into a genuine one. "Your 'friend' had a few good leads for us, and just so you know, I would not have stabbed him." Then he stayed silent, making Brianna feel like she was pulling teeth to get a bit of information.

Taking the bait, she walked over to the map. "I'm glad to hear that. What did you find out? Did he decipher any of these riddles?"

Nathan answered, his excitement at making progress toward the treasure overriding the last of his previous anger. "He made a few changes to the Gaelic translations that I did. It gives a few of them a completely different meaning when including nuances and local idioms that I was unaware of. That was really helpful, but only one riddle sparked a memory of his."

Nathan pointed to a post-it note beside the map that held the translation to the riddle nearest to it.

Brianna reread it:

"The water ripples and turns.

The wulver churns.

Their bones change to flour,

Even the brave do cower."

After she read the note and looked up, Nathan continued, "Lewis was telling me about how the locals love their Scottish folklore. They even host a Folklore Festival every year that's coming up in a few weeks. Even though we know this stuff isn't real, maybe we should look into it more to find the gems of truth hidden beneath the fantasy."

She looked at him with her arms crossed over her chest. "We knew the wulver had to do with folklore from our own research. How does that help us make heads or tails of this map?"

Pleased at her question, Nathan smiled as his voice took on the cadence of a storyteller. "Lewis told me the tale of a cursed man who turned into the wulver. The story goes that he was a spoiled only child of a rich merchant. A beggar and her child came to him asking for a bit of his lunch one day, and instead of sharing, he spit on them. When he woke the next morning, his facial features had turned furry, and he had grown large fangs, while the rest of his body remained human. He was not a werewolf, but it was kind of the same idea. The worst of his problems was that he hungered not for bread awaiting him for breakfast, but for human flesh. In fear for his family's lives, the wulver ran off into the woods. When he could no longer contain the animal growing within, he ended up killing a local miller and lived alone in his mill, where he supposedly ground his victim's bones into flour."

Brianna winced at the story, and Nathan paused for a few seconds. "I know that's a bit of a gruesome tale, but I wanted you to hear it because it explains the riddle. The story is obviously not true, but the mill is an actual place. As a young boy, Lewis and his friends dared each other to go near it, but it had lain vacant for as long as he could remember and none of them would dare approach what was left of the dilapidated building. It's along a river only a handful of miles from here. Lewis told me how to find it but was kind of vague about the exact distance, so I'll have to look it up on a map to be sure. I thought maybe tomorrow we should go check it out."

Brianna's eyes widened at the upcoming adventure. "Finally, a lead!"

Then she paused and looked at him, full of concern. "Did you really threaten Lewis over me? You know there was nothing there, right? I mean, we've only been in Scotland a handful of days."

Nathan smiled. "I was just showing him the sword on the wall that he had admired. We were having a really friendly chat before you came in. I think it was your look of murder toward me that sent him scurrying off."

Brianna ignored his last comment. "Did he have any more insights?"

"Well, you know how there are five creatures drawn on this map? He feels they are all representative of the different Scottish creatures. Looks like we need to brush up on our Scottish folklore, and then we can go hunting the wulver."

Chapter 11

Friendly Neighborhood Babysitter

Brianna

Brianna woke up warm and cozy. Nathan was spooning up against her, with his powerful arms wrapped around her, cuddling. She felt so safe and comfortable. She really loved this man. Out of the corner of her eye, she saw movement. That must have been what awakened her.

Jenna jumped up on the gigantic bed and then squeezed her body between them to fit herself into the previously nonexistent space between Nathan and Brianna. Nathan turned and went back to sleep. Jenna confided in Brianna, "I was scared. I heard a noise downstairs. Last night, I left a bowl of milk out in the kitchen. Do you think it was the brownies?"

Brianna yawned and hugged the little girl. Neither of them wanted to leave the warm bed. "Don't worry, I'm sure it was nothing. Brownies aren't real, but if it would make you feel better, we can go down and check it out together."

Jenna nodded, but Brianna didn't move. She shut her eyes and drifted off back to sleep. After a few minutes, Jenna got antsy and wiggled around, jerking Brianna back to reality. "What do we get to explore today? Can we go see the Loch Hernessy Monster?"

Brianna answered, "I can ask your father about taking a trip to see the loch soon. Today, he actually made plans for you to meet a new babysitter. I'm sure you two will have lots of fun. It's Florine. Do you remember having a conversation about how people from different places speak differently? That's the woman who came to the castle with homemade brownies and you told your daddy she spoke funny."

When Nathan had informed her he made plans to have Florine watch Jenna, Brianna was flabbergasted. Before she became Jenna's governess, he had questioned her about her life, ran a full background check on her without permission, and dug deeply into her online social media presence. *Florine just waltzes up to the house in a promiscuous outfit, handing out sweets, and Nathan falls all over himself to do whatever she wants.*

She was upset, but Nathan seemed so confused by her response that she eventually calmed down. He was trying. After plastering on a fake smile, she thanked him for arranging some adult time. She would try to play nice too.

Brianna climbed out of bed and groaned as the cold air hit her. She wrapped a shawl around herself and put an extra one of Nathan's sweatshirts on Jenna. It was too big, but it would keep her warm. "Let's go check out the kitchen and see what those brownies have been up to. Then we can start making breakfast. The smell of bacon ought to wake up your father."

The two tiptoed quietly down the stairs and into the kitchen. Sure enough, there was a bowl of milk sitting on the floor that something had spilled. All the milk was missing. Jenna ran over excitedly. "There is a brownie living in the castle! Now that I fed him, I wonder if he will clean up my toys if I leave them out!"

Brianna smiled, but she puzzled over the bowl of milk. *How am I going to convince Jenna that brownies don't exist now? I hope we don't have rats!* Not wanting to alarm Jenna over her fears, she thought maybe Jenna would enjoy the pretend play for right now. She would talk to Nathan about it since he was so sensitive to Hector saying anything to her about the local folklore. "Keep in mind that brownies are just make-believe, but if he were real, I'm sure the poor little fellow would have plenty to do sweeping this big old castle. Let's take care of our things and not give him more work to do."

Brianna started breakfast as Jenna sat at the table designing something for the brownie. Sure enough, when the bacon started sizzling, Nathan made his way into the kitchen. He looked so handsome, even with his hair tousled about and sleep shirt wrinkly and slightly askew. Nathan walked up behind Brianna, wrapped his arms around her, and kissed the back of her neck.

Brianna swatted him away. "Excuse me! I'm trying to cook your breakfast!" Quietly she added, "Besides, Jenna is right there."

Nathan smiled at her mischievously but moved away. "It's good for her to see a loving relationship in action." He turned and greeted Jenna. "Good morning, Little Bird. How did you sleep?"

Jenna excitedly showed him the bowl. "Look, Daddy! Brownies are real! They drank the milk I left out for them last night! I'm going to name him Bob. Bob the brownie."

Nathan looked at Jenna and then at Brianna's wide eyes. They both watched to see what he would say. "Those pesky little critters drank all of my milk!" Jenna giggled.

At first, he frowned, but it quickly dissipated and was replaced by a more neutral expression as he sat down at the table with her. "Jenna, I want you to remember that all of this folklore stuff may seem fun, but it is all pretend. There is much more of it around this area than I ever imagined, so we can play along with the locals, as long as we remember that it's all just a fairytale. Do you understand?"

Jenna nodded and went back to studiously drawing a brownie. Nathan pulled out a map of the local area, circled and labeled an area "wulver waterwheel," and plotted a course on where to park and best approach the building. Brianna breathed a sigh of relief that they were on the same page with Jenna. At least there was one argument they didn't need to have. Brianna wondered, did the locals actually believe in these far-fetched stories or just pretend for fun like she and Nathan were telling Jenna to do?

A few hours later, everyone dressed and was ready for the day. Brianna heard a knock at the door, and she hurried to answer it. She wanted a few words with Florine before they left. Brianna opened the door but didn't recognize the woman standing there. The woman had dark braided hair, a strong flowery perfume, and a long conservative old-fashioned floral-patterned dress. She stood beaming at Brianna.

"Hello!" A nasal voice greeted her. Apparently, this was Florine. She had only seen her briefly that one night. Even so, this looked like a totally different woman. Politely, Florine added, "I am so excited to watch your little darling Jenna. I have some fun things planned for the two of us to do today. You and your husband are such a charming couple. Go have some time together. This is your honeymoon, after all! And don't worry about hurrying back. Take your time. I have a lot of experience with children."

Totally thrown off guard, Brianna didn't know what she wanted to say anymore. She definitely couldn't give her a stern talking to now. Confused by the abrupt change in persona, Brianna mumbled, "Hi. Thanks for coming. Nathan and Jenna are in the drawing room. Nathan is making some last-minute plans for our day today."

Brianna led the way. Florine's eyes lit up and eyebrows rose when she noticed the maps laid out on the table. "Are those the famous maps that you were talking about? Mind if I look?"

Nathan saw her enter the room and answered, unfazed by her change in appearance, "These are copies of the map, not the original, but sure, come and look. Maybe you will see something that we haven't been able to decipher."

Florine looked over the map eagerly. After a few minutes, she leaned over the table toward Nathan and thrust her chest out. Brianna wondered if maybe she forgot that her voluptuous breasts weren't currently showing. She looked up at Nathan with her lower lip slightly protruding. "I'm sorry, this is too complicated for me. You must be really smart to understand any of it."

She looks ridiculous. Does she really think that act will work on Nathan?

Nathan awkwardly patted her shoulder. "Now, now. Puzzles, riddles, and maps aren't for everyone."

Apparently, she isn't acting ridiculous enough.

Nathan turned to Brianna. "I'm ready. We can head out now. Jenna, do you want to show Miss Florine your room and the toys we brought from our island?"

Nathan hugged Jenna and gave her a kiss on the cheek. "We will see you in a few hours, Little Bird. You be good for Miss Florine."

Jenna nodded her head. "Did you bring more brownies?"

Florine gave a high-pitched nasally laugh. "As a matter of fact, I did. I brought a few things for us to do today too."

Jenna led Florine out of the room. "Do I get the brownies before or after I do the activities?"

After seeing Jenna settled, Nathan and Brianna got into their car and headed out to the watermill. They followed a main road that followed the shoreline. The dark blue water sparkled in the sunlight and stretched all the way to the horizon, but sheer cliffs made it all inaccessible.

Eventually, they had to turn off onto an unkept dirt road. They didn't make it as far as she hoped when a downed tree made it impossible to continue. Nathan parked. "I guess it's on foot from here. According to this map, it's about a mile and a half walk from here to the old mill. Hopefully, we will find something useful there."

Brianna brought out her backpack. She had packed it with sandwiches, drinks, and a copy of the map. There had to be some kind of reason the map would send them here. Maybe the treasure was here, but there were so many other things on the map that they didn't understand. She had a feeling this was just the beginning.

Nathan and Brianna walked companionably through the forest. Brianna asked Nathan, "What do you think a wulver looks like? I mean, if it were real."

Nathan replied, "From what I read and Lewis confirmed, the Scottish people believe it is just like a man but has a furry wolf's face. What I picture in my head kind of reminds me of the Egyptian gods that had animal faces and human bodies." He picked up a large, long stick that he used as a walking stick. He smiled at her. "Don't worry, I'll protect you."

Brianna smiled back. "If a wulver attacks us, I'll just throw him your sandwich to eat as I run away. See, I can take care of myself."

It was exciting to think about what they might find at the mill. The old giant trees towered above them while the ground was littered with ferns, moss, and small shrubs. Birds chirped gaily. They caught sight of a small red-furred squirrel with tufts on its ears scurrying up a tree. At another point, a large red deer bounded out of the brush near them, scaring Brianna out of her wits. It was a kind of paradise all on its own. Like home, but different. It reminded Brianna of her time learning the traps and puzzles of Riley's Paradise Island.

Finally, they heard the sounds of a river rushing. They spotted a small stone building with moss covering the walls. Whatever roof it once had was long gone. There was a waterwheel in the water, but it looked so old and rotted that it no longer turned. *Has the weather worn away any clues?*

They approached the front entrance. The door had long ago fallen off. Nathan tested the front step to see if it would support his weight. Suddenly, something furry charged out of the building. Right toward them.

Chapter 12

Predatory Babysitter

Brianna

T he animal darted by them into the woods. Brianna's heart pounded as Nathan calmly remarked, "I think that may have been a European fox. I think we are disturbing his den. Let me make sure there aren't any kits in there before we proceed." Brianna glared at him for not being scared out of his wits like she was.

Nathan used his walking stick and spoke softly as he slowly entered the building. There were weeds and small shrubs growing right out of the floor of the building. They found large round mill stones, but they had fallen to the ground. Everything had rotted around them.

Nothing stood out or looked out of place to Brianna. Nothing looked like it had anything to do with the map or privateers. It just looked like an old broken-down building that people told scary stories about.

Brianna got out her copy of the map and read the poem that had brought them here.

"The water ripples and turns,
The wulver churns.
Their bones change to flour,
Even the brave do cower."

Brianna went outside and studied the waterwheel from all angles that she could see. Then she came inside and looked at the millstones. They were too heavy for her to move. Nathan came over to help, but they still wouldn't budge. Regardless, they looked like regular worked stone to her. They sure didn't look like anything out of the ordinary. Nathan poked around at the walls and lifted loose floorboards.

Brianna walked around for a bit, not knowing what else to do. Letting out a shriek, her foot went through a rotten floorboard. From her new lower vantage point, she caught sight of something odd on the far wall. Nathan helped her climb out of the hole.

She brushed all the dirt and debris off of herself, making sure she was intact. A nail had caught on her pants and snagged it slightly, but she considered it a success compared to the rate of ruined clothing she usually went through when adventuring with Nathan.

Brianna bent her knees and hunched down as low as she could, staring at the wall that caught her eye. Nathan looked at her quizzically. "What are you doing?"

Nonchalantly, Brianna answered, "I'm cowering, like in the poem." Then she exclaimed in excitement.

Brianna walked over to one of the stone walls. She pointed to a symbol that was etched into the stone close to the floor. It was mostly covered in moss and only truly apparent from close to the ground. "It's a symbol from the map!"

Brianna gently scraped at the symbol that looked like a wave with a serpent sticking out. The rock was loose. Brianna jiggled the rock, but it was stuck from dirt and the building settling. Nathan took a pointy stick to lever the rock out. By patiently pulling the rock a bit at a time, they could get it out. Behind it were three darkly tarnished silver coins.

"Treasure! Jenna will be so excited when we show her. We found pirate treasure!" Brianna felt giddy. *I can now claim that I have successfully found pirate treasure. Just call me treasure-hunter Brianna!*

Brianna let a daydream reel run through her head where she traveled the oceans finding lost treasures. *Chee Chee chattered upon her shoulder as their ship sailed eastward. Her first mate handed her a spyglass. "Captain, did you really find the lost city of Atlantis? Only you could have figured out the clues in Plato's works to find the real thing..."*

Nathan interrupted her reverie. "These coins are pretty neat, but they are only silver. Technically, it isn't pirate treasure either. If this map is truly from Captain Kiddle like we believe, then it's the hidden earnings of a privateer. I wonder why he would have hidden it here?"

What a spoilsport.

Brianna glared at him. "True, it may be from a privateer, but just because the Scottish royalty said it was okay to steal from their enemies, that doesn't mean they didn't still plunder and kill people. He was hardly different from a pirate, he just had permission to be a pirate." *He may have taken the shine off of my imaginary meanderings, but at least I won't have to resort to using the chocolate coins I bought Jenna now.*

Brianna did a quick internet search on her phone. The coins were probably worth a few hundred to a few thousand altogether. A nice chunk of change to her but a drop in a bucket to Nathan. They would have to get them appraised to be sure.

Regardless of their value, it was the fact they found them on their treasure hunt that made them extra exciting. Now they could call this honeymoon a success... or at least the treasure hunt a success. They would have to see if they could work things out in their relationship before counting the honeymoon as a success.

Brianna and Nathan made their way back to the castle over an hour later. Hector was pulling weeds in one corner of the courtyard. He was minding his own business but intently watching Florine and Jenna. Florine and Jenna were having a tea party in the courtyard when Jenna spotted them. Jenna threw herself at Nathan, telling him how much she had missed him.

"How was your day, Jenna?" Brianna asked.

Jenna brightened up. She ran over to Florine and showed them her teacup. "We had so much fun! We had a tea party and colored and did races and played with my toy ponies. In a disappointed voice, Jenna added, "Miss Florine doesn't think that we have brownies in our house…"

Impressed, Brianna wondered if she had misjudged Florine. She'd only met her for a little. Maybe she should give her another chance. Jenna continued, "… she thinks we have a bogle instead. Miss Florine said that a bogle is kind of like a ghost that likes to trick and confuse people." Brianna groaned. Now Jenna was going to be afraid of ghosts in their castle.

Mind like a gnat, Jenna changed the subject. "Did you guys find the pirate treasure? Was there a dragon? Did you get me a crown of gems?"

Nathan chuckled. He dug into his pocket and pulled out the three coins. "We found a bit of pirate treasure. Although, there was only a fox guarding it, not a dragon. There wasn't a crown, but we will keep on looking."

Florine's eye didn't leave the coins. "When can I watch Jenna next? She is such a sweet darling. Would you like me to come back tomorrow?"

Nathan thought for a moment. "I believe we promised my Little Bird a family trip tomorrow. Would next Wednesday work for you?"

Florine smiled as her eyes followed the coins that Jenna was now examining. Brianna still couldn't make herself trust this woman no matter how hard she tried. Florine answered simply, "I'll be here."

Chapter 13

Meeting the Loch Hernessy Monster

Brianna

Jenna ran along the bank of Loch Hernessy. Sometimes she tripped over the roots of the large trees that hung overhead, but she always bounced right back up. She was too excited to stop. "Where is the Loch Hernessy Monster? I don't see her."

Nathan chuckled. "I don't think she's real, honey. She's just folklore, like the brownies and bogles."

Eventually, they got back in their car and made their way to the Uhart Castle ruins. There were quite a few other tourists there, but not much of the castle remained. Jenna climbed up onto some of the enormous boulders. She shaded her eyes as she looked out over the large body of water. "Is that the Loch Hernessy monster out there?"

Brianna shaded her eyes and looked too. "I'm sorry, honey, I think that's just a boat."

Only a bit of the foundational stones remained of a once giant tower. Jenna skipped back and forth through a lone archway that was connected to a small section of wall.

Her imagination took over. "It's like a doorway that takes you back in time! Quick, jump through before the pirates get you!" She squealed with glee as both Brianna and Nathan hurriedly crossed the threshold. Jenna used the back of her hand to pretend she was wiping sweat off of her brow. "Whew, that was close, but we made it."

They set up a picnic lunch in the shade of the tower ruins, overlooking the loch. It was so breathtaking that even Jenna sat quietly munching on her lunch and overlooking the horizon. Back in the day, it would have been spectacular to live up in that tower and look out the window to see this every morning. Or was the tower where an evil lord kept a damsel in distress? This place was so steeped in history that Brianna couldn't help it when her imagination took off on a wild ride. *I will have to see if I can find out some more about the history of this place.*

Afterwards, they drove to a large beach along Loch Hernessy. The water was chilly, but Jenna got to work busily building a sandcastle. They had a fantastic view of the loch. Periodically, Jenna would look at the lake and squint her eyes but went back to work when there was no sign of an enormous creature.

Brianna sat in the sand next to Nathan. "We have been all over the main tourist areas of Loch Hernessy. The symbol of a woman with hooves was on the map near this area, but now that we're here, I saw nothing out of the ordinary that has to do with the map. We can't search every foot of this giant lake. Any ideas?"

Nathan shook his head. "I didn't see any signs either. Maybe Captain Kiddle had a personal connection with this castle that had nothing to do with the map."

Nathan pulled a copy of the map out of his back jeans pocket. "I mean, the castle we are staying at has a picture of the little man, the brownie, near it, but we haven't seen anything out of the ordinary there. It's possible that some of the clues were worn away, broken into, or previously found. Think about how many people were at Uhart Castle just today. I find it hard to believe that we would find something there when millions of people have walked through what is left of a few pitiful ruins."

Brianna looked over at the map and dejectedly agreed. "I guess you're right. I was just hoping to find another clue today. We have been really puzzling over this riddle near the top of the map."

Brianna read the riddle out loud for Nathan. "'*Black hooves and pools deep. Heedless, she falls beneath. Fair skin she bequeath, leaving wives to weep.*'"

Brianna looked at a map of the area for a while as Jenna happily finished her castle. Then she tapped on Nathan's arm and showed him a point on the map not too far from where they were. "Hey, Nathan, look at this. There is a waterfall in a forest near here. I looked up the kelpie that Hector referred to a while back. It's a black water horse that turns into a deadly woman with black hooves for feet. What if that riddle refers to the waterfall that she lives beneath?"

Nathan gave her a wide grin. "The hunt is on again! I think we should check it out. Jenna, honey, finish up your castle. We're going to find a waterfall next."

After cleaning Jenna up, the trio got into their car and drove to a large sign that read "The Falls of Boyer." They parked in a small lot and walked about half a mile on a well-beaten path.

They passed a couple, who nodded their heads at them in greeting. "The falls are pretty low today, but still pretty." While it had stormed almost the entire first week they arrived, things had been pretty dry since then.

Nathan nodded his head in return. "Thanks for the heads-up. Jenna, there might not be much of a waterfall, but we're almost there, so we're going to check it out anyway."

It wasn't much longer until they could hear the rushing of falling water. They stopped and watched the cascade of water falling over the rocks. It was still magnificent and made Brianna want to come back after a big rainstorm came through.

Jenna lay on her stomach on a large rock and splashed in the water. It was freezing cold. Nathan and Brianna searched around on the rocks. Brianna looked over and saw that Nathan was taking his shirt off.

"I guess I'm checking out the rocks by the falls," Nathan told Brianna.

Brianna looked down at the deep, dark, freezing pool in front of them. A shiver went down her spine just at the thought of going in there. "Don't do it. It's going to give you hypothermia, and the water is so dark. I don't believe in kelpies, but if I did, that's where they would wait for you. Stay out here. Please."

Nathan shrugged. "It will only be for a few minutes. If I don't go in, we will wonder if we missed something. I'll be fine." He gave her a lingering kiss. "I'm glad you care so much."

Brianna grumbled her reply. "I'm not jumping in to save you."

Nathan jumped into the water, making an unmanly yelp at the cold. Then he swiftly swam over to the falls. Brianna could see him running his hand along the rock, feeling his way behind the falls. So far, she had seen nothing else swimming in the dark pool, but she kept her eyes peeled, just in case.

Nathan swam back to shore, a look of triumph in his eyes. "I think I found something. I found a symbol carved into the rock. It felt like a horse. There was a kind of indent in the rock next to it. I think whatever was hidden here is gone."

Disappointed, Brianna helped Jenna up, and the three of them walked swiftly back to the car. There was a blanket in the trunk and Brianna wanted to get Nathan wrapped up in it as soon as possible. It was a pleasant enough day, but Nathan was shivering in his wet pants and had lost most of the normal pep to his step.

When they reached the car, Brianna got the exhausted Jenna settled in the back seat. Then she opened the trunk and a strong whiff of a familiar perfume immediately hit her nose. Confused, she pulled out the blanket, and a woman's bra fell on the ground. An undergarment that didn't belong to Brianna.

Brianna walked to the front of the car, where Nathan was leaning against the hood. She threw the blanket at him and held up the bra. "Who does this belong to?"

Nathan's eyes grew wide as he stammered. "I... I... I don't know how that got in there. It isn't what it looks like."

Brianna glared at him and cut him off. "I don't think I can believe anything you say right now. When we get back to the castle, I'm moving into my own room."

Chapter 14

How to Trap a Brownie

Brianna

Brianna sat with her arms crossed, staring out the passenger window of the car. She turned her whole body away from Nathan, and a single tear trickled down her cheek. What happened to her perfect love story? Did Nathan finally tire of their bickering and find solace in the arms of another woman?

Jenna slept heavily in the backseat. She was so tuckered out from their active day exploring Loch Hernessy that her eyes had shut before they were out of the waterfall's parking lot. Nathan ran his hand through his hair. "Brianna, I seriously don't know how that undergarment got in our trunk. Are you sure it's not yours?"

"Nathan, do you really think I wouldn't recognize it? I need some time to myself to think." Should she believe Nathan or what her own eyes told her was really going on?

"But, Brianna..."

Brianna shook her head but didn't look away from the window. "I don't want to talk to you right now." Nathan let out a heavy sigh, and they rode the rest of the way home in icy silence.

When they arrived back at the castle, Nathan carried Jenna up to her bed to get her settled for the night. Brianna grabbed a few necessities and moved into one of the empty bedrooms that had its own private bathroom. She was too tired and upset for a drawn-out argument about her moving into another bedroom.

As soon as she shut the door, Brianna released the floodgate of tears. She wasn't a big crier, but that night, she couldn't help it. How could she trust him after this? Where did she recognize that perfume from?

Florine.

Before long, Brianna heard a knock on her door. Nathan said, "Brianna? Are you in there? We need to talk about this. You're jumping to conclusions."

Not wanting him to see her this way, Brianna took a few deep breaths to steady her voice. She spoke loudly through the wooden door. "Nathan, I'm not some floozy you can just throw to the side whenever someone shakes their breasts at you. I don't care if you're rich or were my employer before this. We're married now."

Brianna heard a thump like Nathan had rested his head against the door. "Brianna, I love you. I would never cheat on you. We will figure this out and you'll soon see I did nothing wrong. Come on back to our bedroom. Please."

Doubt cleared away Brianna's tears, but it also still clouded her mind. She truly didn't know what to think anymore. "It was a long day. I'm going to sleep in here tonight, and we can talk about it tomorrow, okay?"

Sharply, Nathan replied, "Fine." She didn't hear from him again.

Too agitated to go right to sleep, she quickly called Mavis. After a few rings, she answered. "Hey. What's up, buttercup? I was just about to sit down for some dinner."

Brianna's tears ran again. "Mavis, I'm so glad I got a hold of you! I found this local woman's bra in my trunk, and Nathan said he doesn't know how it got there. He says I'm jumping to conclusions, but he didn't have an explanation for how the bra got in our vehicle. How is my husband being in possession of someone else's undergarments jumping to conclusions? What should I do?"

Mavis interrupted. "You poor thing. I've never heard you this upset before. It was hard to understand everything over all the tears, but if Nathan has cheated on you, I will personally hunt him down. I've got your back, but before you do anything rash, is it possible that Nathan is telling the truth? Is there another explanation for how it got there?"

Brianna gave an enormous sigh. "Oh, I don't know anymore. I've never left something like that lying around in someone else's car. I feel like Florine is up to no good, but the real question is, how involved is Nathan in all of this? You know what? I'm going to bed. I'm so tired I'm falling asleep on the phone. I can't wait until you can come here in person. Things have been so hard lately, and I need my best friend."

"All right. You get a good night's sleep, but make sure you call me tomorrow so I know you're okay. It won't be much longer until I'm there, and we will make that week count. We can even stay up all night talking about every little thing that's been going on if you need to. Good night."

"Good night."

Brianna slipped into a nightgown and went right to sleep. She must not have been getting enough deep sleep at the castle because she'd felt so tired over the last few days. It must have been all the talk about bogles and brownies. That night, she tossed and turned with disturbing dreams of a wingless dragon chasing her through the woods toward the sea. She huffed as she ran with all of her might. Her goal was in sight when she felt hot breath upon her neck...

The next day, Brianna avoided Nathan. She felt better as the morning sunlight streamed through her window, but she still didn't know what to say to him. She didn't want to be made a fool by blindly believing Nathan when the proof pointed elsewhere, but one thing was nagging at her.

When would he have had time for a fling? He had been with either her or Jenna almost the entire time they had been there. He had to jump on to a few work meetings and sometimes he was working early in the morning or late at night in the drawing room, but he hadn't left the castle without her knowledge. Even for a walk.

Brianna snuck out of the new bedroom she'd set up for herself. *The coast looks clear. No sign of Nathan.* She walked quietly to the kitchen to grab a snack for breakfast. She was tiptoeing down the stairs when Nathan came out of the drawing room and spotted her.

A range of emotions from humor to sadness flitted across his face. Stoically, he said, "I found a scholar willing to sell me a few old books about the local area, history, and folklore. He said they should be here in a week or two."

Abruptly, he turned around and headed back into the drawing room. *Hopefully, he stays in there the rest of the day. I need a little more time alone.* As soon as that thought permeated Brianna's mind, Jenna hopped down the stairs after her. *Looks like she's finished playing in her room.*

Cheerfully, Jenna greeted her. "Hello! I'm hungry. Can I have cookies and explore the castle?"

Brianna smiled at the little girl and gave her a hug when they both descended the last stair. "Why don't we get you a bit of a healthier breakfast and you can have a cookie for dessert? I'm getting myself something too." Brianna paused and got down eye to eye with Jenna. She spoke to her seriously. "You're welcome to go exploring, as long as you remember the rules. What did your daddy say about wandering around?"

Jenna recited, "I am not allowed past any of the caution tape because it's dangerous."

Brianna nodded, satisfied. "Yes, that's correct. Let's make something to eat and then you can go explore for a while. Just remember, I'm going to be checking in on you now and again. Follow the rules or you lose your chance to explore by yourself."

The two walked into the kitchen. Jenna hopped up into a large chair while Brianna pulled out some bananas, veggies, and a muffin for each of them. She added a cookie to Jenna's plate. A copy of the treasure map was laid out on the table from the last time she and Nathan were looking over it. Before the trip to Loch Hernessy. Before their big fight.

Brianna sat down at the table to eat. She ached at the thought of losing all that she had gained over the last year and decided not to make any rash decisions. What she needed was to think through a way that she could prove one way or the other if Nathan was guilty or innocent. She had no ideas.

Maybe she needed a distraction to get her mind off all the worry. That sometimes helped her to think more clearly. She pulled the treasure map closer to herself and ruminated over it while she chewed. *If I focus on the treasure map, that will keep my mind busy.*

Jenna got up, placed her dishes in the sink, and scampered off. Brianna focused on the riddle that had a picture of a small dirty-looking man beside it. It was rather close to the castle. Hector had mentioned that this was brownie country, and Lewis identified the small picture on the map as a brownie, but what did it mean? *All this research is just making me crave chocolate.* Brianna read the riddle aloud to herself, then pondered each part.

"*Helpful yet complex, troublesome when vexed. Look into the hearth, treasure from the Earth.*"

Hmm... that's interesting. It couldn't hurt to look at the hearths of the castle. Even if it didn't lead to anything, she figured it would give her something to focus on for an hour or two. She was looking for a distraction. This would be perfect.

Brianna started at the kitchen hearth. As the focal point of the household, it seemed the most obvious place, and she was already there. She carefully looked over all the bricks surrounding the fireplace and swept away as much soot as she could to examine the inner firebox. Nothing.

Then she worked her way through the fireplaces in each of the bedrooms. In the last spare bedroom, Brianna opened the door and stepped into the room. Her bare foot landed right in a bowl of milk and a basket fell on her head. She sighed. So, this was what Jenna was working on. Instead of just feeding the brownies, it looked like she was trying to catch them now too. *She definitely has the Riley genes.*

Brianna cleaned up the brownie trap and checked every inch of the hearth inside and out. There was no sign of anything out of the ordinary. Brianna dreaded it, but the last fireplace to check was the drawing room. *Can I make it in and out without talking to Nathan?*

Brianna soundlessly opened the door to the drawing room and peeked inside. Nathan looked totally engrossed in a map. Perfect. Brianna silently made her way over to the fireplace that, thankfully, wasn't lit. She examined the floor of the fireplace. She was just about to sneak back out of the room when she caught sight of Nathan staring right at her.

"You had no right to take my notebook." Nathan's sharp voice made her wince. How dare he take that tone with her?

"I never touched your notebook. You probably misplaced it."

Exasperated, Nathan ran his hand through his hair. "Brianna, I told you. Nothing happened, but I think I figured out what's going on. Before we left to go to the wulver's mill, Florine asked to borrow a blanket for a picnic with Jenna. When we got home, I saw it wrapped in a ball by the doorway and just threw it in the car. I didn't know the bra was in there."

Brianna's eyes narrowed. "That still doesn't explain why her bra was in there in the first place. I think we should question her. That's not something a woman just takes off at random."

Nathan shrugged. "You women are always complaining about how uncomfortable those things are. Maybe it just got itchy. What do you have against her, anyway? She helped you out when we arrived here and took the time to bring us a welcome gift." Nathan looked at Brianna with his brows furrowed in confusion and frustration. "She is supposed to come and watch Jenna in a few days, and honestly, from the way things are going right now, we could use the time alone together now more than ever."

At the last word, Brianna spun around and left in a hurry. She was unaccustomed to choking back tears, but lately, it felt like she was tearing up over everything. *How dare he? How could he take that woman's side over hers?*

Chapter 15

Castle of Secrets

Brianna

Brianna was so mad at Nathan that she stomped up the stairs, planting a bare foot directly into a pile of soot. Handily, there was a broom placed right beside the now scattered ashes. Brianna looked around. There was a cookie on the floor underneath an upside-down garbage can. Something would easily knock over the stick holding it in place when someone reached for the cookie. Brianna cleaned up this brownie trap and stopped in her bathroom to clean her feet.

Feeling a lot calmer, she went to find Jenna. *This has to stop.* Since the little girl wasn't in the bedrooms or the drawing room, Brianna tried the kitchens. As soon as she walked through the door, her jaw dropped as she stopped to take everything in. Brianna found Jenna working busily. She had a pile of breadcrumbs on the floor and string zigzagging across the kitchen from the chairs to the cupboards.

Jenna saw her and proudly explained while she continued to work. "Do you like my trap? This one will tangle up the brownie for sure. I set up three other traps. The first trap I made got all cleaned up! That was the brownie at work. I almost had him. This trap will get him, though."

Brianna saw how proud she was of her invention and didn't want to disappoint the little girl. "Jenna, honey, I think your trap is very impressive. I think it definitely would catch a brownie if we had one.

Unfortunately, the other ones you set, I stepped in and cleaned up, not the brownie. We can't have these traps all around the castle, but I have an idea for a compromise. What if we designate one area where you can build all the traps you want, and I will leave it alone?"

Jenna eyed her masterpiece across the kitchen and looked at Brianna suspiciously. "Can my trap area be in the kitchen?"

Brianna wanted to bang her hand against her head. Was this how Nathan and his brother had started? Was Jenna going to add to the family's favorite pastime? Instead, she calmly replied, "Unfortunately, honey, this isn't a great place for traps. We need to cook and eat in here. How about we move it to one of the spare bedrooms?"

Jenna hung her head and replied in a defeated tone. "All right, I'll start taking it down. I might miss the brownie while I'm moving it, though."

Brianna helped Jenna clean up while her mind thought again about the riddle. She wondered what was in the east and west wing. They were caution-taped off, and she knew Nathan wouldn't be pleased if she explored there alone, but right then, she didn't care. She would be careful. Maybe there was a hearth she hadn't explored.

Jenna scampered off to claim a spare bedroom while Brianna went exploring. On her way to the west wing, she spotted a third trap. Jenna sure had a busy morning. At *least I spotted this one before being caught in it. I finally outsmarted a six-year-old*. She'd positioned this trap a few feet in front of the caution tape.

There was a note with phonetically spelled words that translated to, "I love you. Fun for you." There was a box that was colored on and decorated with crayon-colored windows. An empty tissue box had a towel over it to look like a bed. There was a small plate with a muffin on it and a glass of milk next to it. I *should have paid more attention when Jenna left after our snack*.

It looked like Jenna had worked very hard on this latest brownie trap. Instead of using a trap to catch him, she was trying to persuade him to stay with comforts. She had to give the girl credit for her ingenuity. Brianna left the brownie house there for the moment. She would have Jenna move it through the house to her new trap room. She would have to talk to her about keeping the food in the kitchen too.

Brianna carefully moved through the caution tape in the west wing, trying not to disturb it. There was dust covering the ground. Curiously, there were a few pairs of footprints that had recently gone down this hallway. *I will have to ask Nathan and Jenna if they came down here past the caution tape.*

The walls looked like they were crumbling in some areas. This wing mostly seemed to be comprised of bedrooms. Some had doorways that led to another bedroom. Some had bedrooms that led to sitting rooms. There were a few antique lamps and lots of dusty, forgotten furniture.

These rooms were bigger and more elaborate than the ones they currently stayed in. She guessed they probably originally belonged to the family who owned the castle. That would make the rooms they were staying in the guest rooms. The smaller rooms must have been an easier place to start renovations.

After a quick peek into the first room, Brianna started a more methodical search of each room. Although in ill repair, nothing looked outright dangerous. She searched the fireplaces of the master bedroom and the adjoining ladies' room. There were half a dozen more rooms that she scoured, but the hearths all looked normal to her. Eventually, she came to what looked like a children's nursery. There were even some low shelves with a few wooden toys covered in cobwebs.

Brianna approached the hearth of the room and looked down at the bricks that lined the bottom. She lifted an old rusty firedog bracket out of the hearth. Underneath was a symbol of an awkward little person with a broom, just like on the map. Hands covered in soot, Brianna jiggled at the brick until it came loose. Underneath was a small, dented, rusty metal box.

Treasure! Brianna removed the metal box and pried open the lid. She found a handful of gems inside. Her inexperienced eye saw common gems that she'd recently taught Jenna about in science class. There was a clear quartz, a purple amethyst, a blue sodalite, and a black onyx. There was also a cut pink gem, maybe rose quartz.

She knew her find would not make her rich, but it thrilled her all the same. Smiling at her success, Brianna eyed her finds for a few more moments. She'd figured out another riddle and now they had more of the hidden treasure. Brianna placed the gems back inside their metal container and slid it into her pocket.

Brianna took a few steps back into the main hallway. *I can't wait to show Nathan and Jenna! Maybe I should believe and forgive Nathan. He really seemed sincere about the bra, even if he was being thickheaded about Florine.* He didn't seem like the type to have a secret affair, but he also really didn't have the opportunity either. She decided to give him a break, but she would also keep her eyes peeled for any suspicious behavior.

Her mind played out the conversation she would have with Nathan. She should apologize for not believing him, but he also should at least acknowledge that it was cruel to call her jealous when she had physical evidence of something weird going on.

All the while, her mind spun, she wasn't paying attention to her feet. Before she knew it, a creature darted away from her foot with a loud, high-pitched yowl. It shocked Brianna so much that she took a step backwards and banged into an old dusty tapestry. She kept falling into blackness.

Chapter 16

Curiosity Killed the Cat

Brianna

B rianna's heart beat loudly in her chest as she panicked. Everything was completely black. She could feel gritty stone beneath her. Brianna stayed on her hands and feet and tried to crawl forward. Her head banged into a stone wall. She felt debris fall into her hair and down her neck.

Her head throbbed horribly, but she had to find a way out of this mess. She put her hand in front of herself and tried a different direction. It felt like there was a thick rug-like material in front of her, and she saw a flash of light. She pushed harder and fell out of the secret passageway.

Hmmm... I wonder where that leads to. She would have to come back and explore further with a flashlight. Brianna looked around to see if she could find what had surprised her. Upon closer inspection, hers weren't the only footprints in this hallway.

There were her footprints and another set of unidentified shoe prints along the center of the hallway. Along the edge of the hallway, she could see tiny paw prints. *Would a brownie have feet or paws?* They seemed to mostly lead to one of the bedrooms that she checked earlier. She carefully walked into the bedroom, senses alert. She heard a soft purring sound.

Brianna followed the soft noise to an old cabinet. She looked underneath to where a pile of rags was lying about haphazardly. There on the blanket was a calico cat. She was lying on her side, eyes closed, and purring contentedly.

Six little blind kittens nursed furiously, crawling over each other to get a better latch. The cat eyed Brianna cautiously but didn't move. Brianna smiled to herself. *Looks like I found our milk-drinking brownie. Won't Jenna be surprised?* She quietly backed away, trying not to disturb the little family.

Brianna made her way back to the main living area of the castle. Her surprise at finding the secret passageway and the cat made her forget about the gems in her pocket. Stomach grumbling, Brianna stopped in the kitchen to grab a snack, but she wasn't quite ready to talk to Nathan. Feeling braver from her adventures in the west wing, curiosity drove Brianna to explore beyond the caution tape of the east wing.

Brianna opened the first door and saw a gigantic room. There was a beautiful but faded painting on the ceiling. It showed hosts of angels dancing and playing music. The floor was a beautiful pattern of alternating cream and brown marble diamonds. There were a few tables leaning against a wall and carts filled with plates and cutlery. It looked to be some kind of entertaining room or ballroom.

She stepped on broken plaster on the cool stone ground. "Ouch!" She really should have grabbed shoes. If only she had planned on traversing the entire castle when she first left her room then she would have dressed appropriately. *Oh, well. Too late now.*

Brianna peeked into the next room on the other side of the hallway to find an extensive library. A large desk and table stood in the middle of rounded walls lined with musty, moth-eaten books. Was this the turret that looked like it was falling from the outside? Brianna longed to get her hands on some books in that room but decided not to enter, just in case it wasn't safe.

The last room was a small chapel. They lined a few pews up in front of a large central cross. Brianna walked into the room and took a few minutes to say, "Thank you for giving me Nathan and Jenna. Please watch over us as we navigate becoming a family." When she left the chapel, she felt a peace settle over her soul. *I think I'm ready to talk to Nathan now.*

Brianna passed a part of the wall that didn't line up one hundred percent correctly. She pulled on the wall, and it opened like a door. If they had shut it the whole way, it would have been nearly impossible to see. The doorway led Brianna up a flight of stairs to a series of rooms with low ceilings. The first room had a single dirty mattress on a tiny bed frame and a small dresser.

Brianna opened the next door, and a mouse scurried across the floor. At least the cat had plenty of food here in the castle. This room had three tiny broken-down beds with small chests at each foot. The last room was the biggest, but it was just lined with eight tiny beds and nothing else. *Looks like I found where the servants stayed. I wonder what they will do with this area when Nathan's aunt renovates it.*

The servants' hallway had an odd picture on the wall of a younger man with red hair and a handlebar mustache. Brianna puzzled over who this man was and found it odd that this fancy-looking portrait would be on the servants' floor.

The servants' floor ended with another stairway. This stairway descended to a door behind the main staircase, near the kitchens. This one also blended in with the wall. *I must have walked past it a hundred times and never even noticed it before.*

Feeling better after her adventures, Brianna made her way to the drawing room. *I will find Nathan and clear the air.* Her stomach rumbled. *Then I will make lunch. Everyone else is probably starving too. I was gone longer than intended. Maybe a few hours.*

Before she could get very far, she ran into Nathan. He sighed in relief and engulfed her in a hug. "There you are! I'm so sorry I talked to you that way. I was out of line." Nathan put his arms on her shoulders, as if he wanted to hug her, but ended up holding her at arm's length. His brows furrowed as his eyes roamed over every inch of her. "We couldn't find you anywhere. I thought maybe you'd left." Brianna looked down at herself and realized she was filthy.

After picking a spiderweb out of her hair, he examined it and asked, "Where *were* you? You always look beautiful to me, but right now, you kind of look like you just crawled out of a rat's nest."

Brianna chuckled. Her adventure had covered her hair in dust and cobwebs. Soot covered her hands and knees that she'd smudged all over her face and, of course, she'd done all of this barefoot. Her feet were completely black.

Brianna wetted her lips and spoke softly. "Thank you for apologizing. I'm sorry I jumped to conclusions about you and Florine. I will try to trust you more." *I will have that conversation with Florine about making sure she watches her step, though. The bra in the blanket must have been some kind of manipulative game she thought she was playing. Unfortunately for her, I don't like those kinds of games, and I refuse to play. Florine will either cut it out or get out.*

Brianna dug in her pocket and brought out the small box of gems. "As for me, I was out treasure hunting!"

She handed it to Nathan, who exclaimed in excitement, "Wow, where did you find this?"

"Let me get cleaned up. Then I can tell you and Jenna all about my adventures over lunch." She paused. "Although, it's pretty late. Did you guys already eat?"

Nathan nodded. "Yeah, I made sandwiches. When Jenna got hungry, we tried to find you, but you weren't anywhere we looked. Your phone rang unhelpfully from your bedroom. I'll whip you up a sandwich if you want." His eyes went wide as he moved closer, despite her dirtiness. "Will you move back into our room? It's so lonely without you. I love you. I miss you."

Brianna laughed. "It's been one night!" Then more seriously, she added, "I love you, and I do believe you about Florine. I also think we have some things to work through if we want this relationship to work." Brianna gave him a soft kiss on the lips and looked him in the eyes. "I've been having a lot of trouble sleeping lately, and I wake up every day exhausted. I think I need to have my space right now so I can get myself back into a good place where I'm feeling better. Maybe if we take a step back, we can figure out how to work together and live together as man and wife. Then everything else will fall into place. I love you. We can make this work, but I need a little time."

Chapter 17

Beihir's Swimming Pool

Brianna

The next morning over a breakfast of eggs, they were having a relaxed conversation. Jenna entertained them with her dreams. "So, then I heard a bell ring that told me my trap went off, and I knew I caught a brownie! I ran as fast as I could to see the little guy because my room was a real mess and I needed his help, but when I got there, I couldn't find a little man anywhere. Instead, a chocolate brownie lay in the trap. I don't know how it got there, but it sure was delicious!"

Brianna and Nathan laughed. This felt natural and comfortable, like their daily life back home on Riley's Paradise Island before they were married. She missed her home so much that it almost made her teary. *What's wrong with me? I'm so emotional lately.*

Nathan gave her a smirk. "Want to go for a walk on the beach?"

Jenna jumped up and down excitedly. "Yes! I would love to go to the beach. I can't wait to play in the sand!"

Nathan winced, then responded to Jenna. "Sorry, Little Bird. We won't have time to play in the sand during this adventure, but we can go back another day to play. Next time, we can take a whole day to just play in the sand and have a picnic on the beach."

Brianna frowned. "What did you have in mind, then? All the beaches around here are inaccessible under those steep cliffs."

Nathan jutted out his chin. "I think I figured out another riddle on the map, but I'm going to leave it a surprise. If we leave soon, we can be at the beach by low tide. We just have to drive down to an old man-made stone staircase I read about a few miles away from here. It goes straight down to the bottom of the cliff to the beach. We should have plenty of time to walk to the base of the cliff nearest our castle and get back to the stairs before the high tide comes in. As long as we don't take time to dally in the sand."

Brianna threw together a bag with some quick lunches and bottles of water and they were ready to go. They drove to the stone stairway. Giant boulders that were weathered with age and moss were placed as the perfect stepping stones to make it safely from the top of the cliff to the bottom. Brianna wondered how the Scotsmen of old had engineered such a thing before the day of big machinery and cranes.

When they made it to the bottom of the stairs, Jenna picked up a pretty stone on the ground. Nathan ushered them on. "We will come back for those. Let's walk now and play with whatever extra time we have before the tide comes in."

Nathan tried to keep them going at a decent clip, but Jenna couldn't help herself. There were rocks that sparkled in the sunshine and rock pools filled with amazing creatures. Jenna was fascinated watching a pair of crabs battling in one pool. She picked up a starfish in another pool to show them and asked about the barnacles she found on some rocks.

Nathan was trying to be encouraging to his inquisitive daughter, but Brianna could tell he was getting frustrated. "Why don't we come back another day to check out whatever it is you want to show us? Jenna is having such a good time."

Brianna could see Nathan internally battling his need to find out if he'd figured out the riddle correctly. Brianna saw him decide and visibly relax. "Okay," he said. "Let's slowly start heading back. Little Bird, let's see what treasures we can find."

Nathan got down and explored the rock pools with Jenna. He pointed out a few fish in one pool. "That one is a type of goby."

Jenna excitedly pointed at a rock pool shrimp. "Look! It's a bug in the water."

"He looks a lot like an insect, but he is actually a crustacean. They are both a type of arthropod, but they're different. Do you see how there are two main parts to his body?"

Jenna nodded, so Nathan drew a picture of an ant in the sand. "Insects have three parts of their body."

That's the man I fell in love with. His family always comes first. I think this is exactly what we needed today.

Jenna reached for a five-legged common starfish. She slipped on some algae and splashed headfirst into the tidal pool. Brianna jumped down into the thigh-high chilly water and scooped her out.

At first, Jenna sputtered in surprise. After she regained her composure, she smiled up at Brianna and giggled. "Oops. I slipped."

Brianna smiled back. "I'm just glad I was there to catch you! Now look at us; we're all wet."

Jenna hugged Brianna, ensuring that the last dry parts of her got wet as well. "Does that mean we can go swimming now?"

Nathan, watching the exchange, took Jenna from Brianna's arms and helped her out of the rock pool. "I don't know about swimming, but luckily, it's a warm enough day that we won't get too cold if we just splash around. I remember seeing a large rock pool pretty close to the stairway. We can play in it for a bit, Little Bird."

Jenna squealed. "Yes, yes, yes! Best Day *ever*!" She squirmed down from her father's grasp and moved steadily down the rocky shore.

Brianna looked at Nathan and hurried after Jenna. "Looks like she can move fast when she wants to. Obviously we didn't motivate her enough earlier."

They stopped at a large rectangular rock pool. The tide was coming back in slightly, but they could easily see the stairway from where they were. It was an easy walk away.

Jenna splashed about, trying to catch a tiny fish. Brianna studied the pool. "Nathan, this doesn't look like it formed naturally. When you read about the staircase, did they say anything about the pool?"

Nathan frowned as he circled the rock pool as much as the rising tide would allow. "I agree. This is too much of a perfect rectangle to be natural. I wonder how they made this. It gets decently deep in the middle and holds water even in low tide." Grinning, he said, "I bet if we asked the locals, they would tell us a story about dwarves carving it. What do you think?"

Brianna smiled, enjoying seeing this playful side of him again. "The beihir is supposed to be a dragon serpent that lives by the ocean, right? I think this is its swimming pool."

An hour later, Jenna finished wading around in the man-made rock pool. The little family slowly made their way the rest of the way back to the stone staircase. They ate their turkey sandwich picnic happily on the bottom step.

It was a perfect day to remember. A bit of paradise in the Scottish Highlands. Brianna savored it. *Will it last?*

Chapter 18

Beihir's Cave

Nathan

Nathan stood sentinel outside of the castle's main door. He really should have gotten Florine's phone number, then he could have called and told her not to come instead of waiting outside to fire her before Brianna saw her. Regardless, he was there because he had to make this right.

The few times he had met Florine, she'd seemed nice enough to him. Could she really be as manipulative and conniving as Brianna thought? *I guess it doesn't matter. Brianna needs me to show her I'm on her side, no matter what.*

Nathan watched a car pull up and park outside the courtyard. Florine flounced down into the courtyard with a basket in hand. *Great, more brownies.* How did one fire a woman who just baked brownies for you? Especially very delicious brownies.

She wore an oddly augmented dress. The main body of the dress looked very conservative, but she'd adapted the bodice to show as much cleavage as possible without falling out.

I guess there were some warnings I should have seen...

Smiling, she bounded up the stairs, her bosom bouncing with each hop. "Nathan! I'm so glad to see you! I can't wait to watch your little darling today." She held up the basket. "I made you brownies again!" Nathan got a whiff of her strong perfume. Brianna was right; it was the same scent that was on the bra.

Nathan ran his hand through his hair. "Look, Florine. I'm sorry to have you come all this way, but things just aren't working out. We are going out today, but we're going to take Jenna with us."

Florine's eyes widened. "Did Jenna not enjoy herself with me last time?"

He was really hoping she would just accept that explanation and walk away. It looked like he would have to do this the hard way.

Nathan ran his hand through his hair again. "No, it's not that. It's that we found one of your undergarments in the picnic blanket you borrowed."

Florine's jaw dropped, and her eyes grew wide. "You couldn't believe that was me!" Her nostrils flared, but it lost some of its effect when he heard her nasal voice. "I take the care of a child seriously. I did not take this job lightly, and I am not one to take my undergarments off willy-nilly!"

Florine dramatically dropped the basket of brownies, turned, and huffed out of the courtyard.

That didn't go well. Was it possible the bra belonged to someone else? *I feel like I should apologize, but I'm not sure to whom, my wife or Florine. I'd better just let it go.*

Out of the corner of his eye, Nathan spotted Hector weeding the courtyard, well within earshot. *When did he get here? For all the weeding that man does, I would expect this courtyard to be spotless.*

Nathan picked up the basket of brownies. He opened up the folded kerchief that covered them. *Those smell delicious. The brownies shouldn't suffer from this petty squabble.* Nathan picked up one of the brownies and took a bite. Perfectly soft and chewy, the dark chocolate melted in his mouth. He decided to eat them in the drawing room out of Brianna's sight, just in case she got the wrong idea.

After making sure that all signs of chocolate were erased, Nathan went to the kitchen. Jenna and Brianna were finishing up packing lunches for the day.

Nathan declared, "Today we will make it the whole way down the beach! Are you girls ready?"

Jenna yelled back and saluted, "Yes, we are, sir!"

Nathan eyed Brianna. "Where did she learn that?"

Brianna shrugged innocently.

Again, they drove down to the stone steps and walked along the sand until they got to the rocky part of the beach. Nathan put Jenna up on his shoulders and led them at a grueling pace past many rock pools.

"I see seals swimming out there!" Jenna called excitedly.

Nathan's shoulders were getting tired, and they still had a decent way to go. He decided this was as good a place as any to stop.

There was an enormous mostly dry rock nearby. They briefly paused to eat their sandwiches as they watched the playful animals dive and bark at one another.

Nathan hoisted Jenna back up on his shoulders as they continued on their way. Finally, Nathan told Brianna, "According to my calculations, we should be pretty close. Since the castle isn't directly against this cliff, there is a wide area that we have to search around here."

"Are you going to tell me what we're looking for yet?" Brianna asked.

Instead of explaining, Nathan pointed. "There!" He picked up his speed even more until he reached the mouth of a small cave. He took Jenna down from his shoulders. "I don't want to bump your head, so you're just going to hold my hand really tight in here, okay?"

Wide-eyed, Jenna replied, "Okay." Then her voice picked up pitch and speed. "Is this the dragon's home? Is this where the treasure is?"

Brianna caught up to Nathan and Jenna. "How neat! How did you find out about this place?"

Nathan proudly explained to them both, "Well, I was thinking about the beihir dragon of Scottish folklore. I wasn't positive there was a cave under here, but there was a picture of a beihir on our treasure map by the shore. The folklore says this serpent lived in a cave. If it was supposed to live around here, there had to be a cave for it to live in, right? We drove by and looked down from the top of the bluffs. I thought it was about time we looked around the bottom."

Nathan dug a flashlight and his copy of the map out of his backpack. They slowly entered the cave. An acrid scent overwhelmed his nose as he saw hundreds of small furry shapes on the roof of the cave. Bats! *Gotta love the smell of guano to clear out one's nose.*

He spoke quietly to Brianna and Jenna, who huddled close to the light. "Make sure you two don't make any sudden loud noises or movements. There are a lot of bats sleeping above us, and we don't want to spook them."

He watched Jenna and Brianna's eyes widen as they looked up. They nodded their heads, not daring to speak, and tiptoed deeper into the cave. Nathan started to slowly and systematically move his flashlight up and down along the walls of the cave. With the tide coming back in soon, he had little time to search. He needed to find a symbol from the map or at least something out of the ordinary. *Come on. Where is the beihir dragon?*

Behind them, Nathan heard a scuffling noise and a small rock fell. He swung the flashlight around but only caught sight of an arm and leg escaping the cave. Dodging stalactites and giving the bats a wide berth, Nathan gave chase. He made his way out of the cave, but unfortunately wasn't fast enough while holding Jenna's hand. By the time he reached the cave mouth, whoever it was, they were long gone.

Someone followed us, but who?

Brianna, close on his heels, looked out at the water. They had moved swiftly, but it already looked higher than before. "Nathan? I think we should head back. It was kind of creepy that someone followed us down here, and I saw nothing in that cave that tied into our treasure hunt. It looks like the tide is getting higher, and I don't want to swim back to the stone staircase. Can we come back another day to search some more?"

Nathan ran his hand through his hair as he went to check on the water himself. He felt like they were so close, and he definitely didn't have time to search the cave thoroughly. He checked the clock on his phone.

He sighed. *Sometimes being responsible is so frustrating.* "Yeah, between walking on the sand and carrying Jenna, it took us longer to get out here than I expected, and I don't want to risk getting stranded. Let's head back for now."

Chapter 19

A Selkie's Skin

Nathan

Nathan hummed as he carried a box to the drawing room. He called down the hallway cheerily, "My books are here! Now we will know everything about the local history and folklore."

Brianna and Jenna followed Nathan to the drawing room that was now his office. Even though he still hummed with excitement, he placed the box down gingerly. Carefully, he opened the box.

He pulled out two thick, old leather tomes. Nathan opened the first book called *Archives of Tober*. This book had a series of old colorful hand-drawn maps of the local area and a biography of the local inhabitants and their descendants.

Nathan glanced through a few pages until he came to the heading Dunam Castle. He skimmed a few pages. The book was fascinating. He couldn't wait until he had more time to sit down and read it more thoroughly. He slowly flipped through the pages... *Aha!*

He read a small section out loud for Brianna and Jenna. "Here's a part about my ancestors... 'A boy by the name of Angus Kiddle was born to Lord Alastair Kiddle and Lady Adeline Dunam. While he was still young, Angus's parents were killed, and the Rallister family took the castle over. Angus stayed on as a servant for many years until he ran away to sea. Angus Kiddle later became the feared privateer Captain Angus Kiddle. The Rallister family was...'" Nathan's eyes sparkled.

"No wonder Kiddle hid those gems in the nursery's hearth. That was *his* nursery."

Nathan's eyes skimmed over the page a bit more until he began reading again. "'While in his late twenties, Angus left on a great expedition to make his fortunes, reclaim his titles, and win the woman he loved, but he was lost at sea.'"

Nathan looked up, and Brianna could hear the awe in his voice. "He didn't just get lost at sea. He must have been stranded on what later became Riley's Paradise Island."

Oblivious to her father's revelations, Jenna started to slowly leaf through the other book called *The Monstrosities of Scotland*. Her eyes were as wide as saucers as she examined each page of beautifully hand-illustrated Scottish folklore creatures.

Nathan hurried to her side. "Careful, Little Bird. The book is very old and expensive, but remember, everything in it is just pretend. Why don't I turn the pages while we look at it together?"

They turned to the page titled Beihir. A beautiful black-and-green serpent with short, scaled legs twisted around the page. Sharp claws and fangs extended as if ready to pounce. Both fierce and beautiful. Nathan read its description aloud.

"'The beihir was a creature that resembled either a serpent with legs or a dragon without wings. It spits acid at its victims that poisons them. The only cure for the acid was for the love of the victim to reach the creature's watery island home before the beihir could return home.'"

Nathan had a look on his face like a lightbulb had just gone off. He went over to the large map he had displayed on the table and read the riddle by the symbol of the beihir.

"'*Fierce fiend of acid. His home contrasted. Beneath and above. A token of love.*'"

Words started to tumble out of his mouth. "I thought the riddle was referring to a cave that was both above and underwater dependent on the tide. That's why we checked out the one under the bluffs near the castle."

Nathan's excitement was so infectious that Jenna jumped up and down. Nathan smiled at her as he spoke. "Do you remember the seals we watched that were playing around that small rock island? What if the riddle is referring to a rock island that's covered up at high tide and appears at low tide? The rock island would be contrasted both beneath and above, depending on the tides!"

He picked up his phone. "Let me make a few calls. Hopefully, we will be on our next adventure in a few days!"

Nathan directed the motorboat toward a rocky outcropping they could see peeking out of the waves at low tide. Jenna sat in the middle of the boat, her life jacket secured around her. "Do you think we will see any seals today?"

Nathan smiled at his daughter. "Maybe. They do love to sun themselves on small rocky islands like the one we're visiting today. Keep your eyes peeled."

A look of concern washed over Nathan's face as he remembered something. He shouted over the sound of the motor. "Brianna, did you happen to take the three silver coins we found?"

Brianna shook her head. "Where did you last leave them?"

"Last I saw them, I put them in a little box on top of the table I turned into my desk in the drawing room. I haven't peeked at them for over a week. This morning, thinking of our treasure hunt, I went to look them over. They were gone."

Eyes slightly narrowing, he looked at Jenna. "Jenna, did you take the coins? You know I told you not to go in that room when I'm not there. Tell me the truth and you won't get in trouble."

Wide-eyed, Jenna replied immediately. "No, Daddy. I didn't take them. I've been too busy in my trap room. If I keep working at it, I know I'll catch *something*."

"Do you think maybe Florine might have taken them while she was watching Jenna?" Brianna asked.

Nathan shook his head. "The last time she watched Jenna is when we found the coins. She wouldn't have had the opportunity. I think it's Hector. I know he's supposed to be the landscaper, but it feels like he's always around just watching. He also has a key to the castle."

Brianna scrunched up her cheeks. *I hope Nathan isn't upset that I never got around to telling him the complete story about my adventures in the off-limits wings. Once I mentioned kittens, that's all Jenna wanted to talk about.*

They were nearing the island, but Brianna still had to shout her next comment over the noise of the motor. "You know, when I was exploring a few days ago and I went into the west wing, there were footprints in the dust already. Someone had recently walked through there."

Jenna shouted, "Seals! I see them! There are three that just jumped in the water!"

Nathan smiled and turned off the motor to float and watch the seals. "Good eyes, Little Bird. Look over there. Their heads popped back up. They're watching us!"

He turned to Brianna. "Are you sure they weren't your own footprints?" Again, he turned to Jenna. "Were you beyond the caution tape?"

Innocently, Jenna shook her head and then went back to watching the seals.

Brianna continued, "More importantly than the footprints, there was this tapestry that covered a secret passageway that I fell into." Brianna looked at him with concern on her face. "What if someone is using a secret door to get into the castle? You never did find your special notebook, and now the coins are missing too. We have also heard more weird things in the castle than a couple of cats would account for."

Nathan looked at her with his mouth hanging open. "You didn't think it was important to tell me about secret passageways in the castle before now? Here I am taking us out into the rocky ocean in a little boat for the sake of adventure, while there was more to figure out in the castle right in front of my nose!"

Brianna shifted uncomfortably. "Well, that was a busy afternoon and I was so excited to tell you guys about the treasure I found that the passageway slipped my mind. I'm sorry, I haven't been sleeping well lately, and my mind feels like a sieve. My brain just feels fuzzy."

With a frown, Nathan studied her for a few moments. "Are you feeling well? We can call around and find a doctor if you think you're coming down with something."

Brianna shook her head. "No, I don't think there is anything wrong, I just feel off. I'm sure once we find this treasure and I'm back to getting a good night's sleep, I'll be fine."

Before long, they arrived at the rocky outcropping. Nathan pulled the boat up next to the shore. He tied a rope to a rock. "You guys stay here. I want to take a little look around."

Nathan walked around the rock. It wasn't big; less than ten square yards. It was covered in bits of moss and lichen, but otherwise bare.

Nothing looked out of the ordinary, and there were no map symbols anywhere that he could see.

He walked back to the boat. Jenna was barking like a seal. He guessed his imaginative little girl was probably trying to communicate in seal language. Brianna's long hair blew wildly around her from the wind. She laughed heartily at Jenna's antics and looked totally at peace.

Look at the beautiful woman. She makes me happy and my heart complete. I was lucky enough to win her over once. I will just have to do it again. I can't screw this up.

Off-handedly, he said to Brianna, "You know, I wish you were one of those mythical women who turned into seals, a selkie. Then you could just slip into the water like a seal and see if you could find any clues to unlocking the secrets of our treasure map."

That woman is about as elusive as a selkie too.

Speaking of selkies... Nathan smiled mischievously. "I have an idea, but I will have to do some research on where you can get training."

Brianna looked at him with her eyes narrowed and brows furrowed. "Training? For what?"

Chapter 20

Selkie in Training

Brianna

Brianna came down to Nathan's drawing room because, over lunch, he told her he had an idea he wanted to pass by her. He was trying to open up the communication between them, and things had been going so well that Brianna was considering moving her things back in with Nathan. Maybe she had been too hard on him by moving to a different bedroom.

The only thing that stopped her was the fact that she still wasn't sleeping well. She was waking up groggy and even needed to take a nap in the middle of the day yesterday to catch up on her sleep. That was totally out of character for her. In fact, these fitful nights of sleep were making her nauseous when she woke up in the morning. She was in no shape to move back in with him until she got herself under control.

Brianna saw Nathan watching her as she entered the room. "Brianna, what if, instead of on top of the rock island, the treasure is under the water of the rock island?"

What is that crazy man getting me into now? "Nathan, if we don't find the rest of the treasure, it's not the end of the world. I don't want to get in over our heads over a silly map. The water is freezing. There are some really strong currents out there and lots of sharp rocks."

Nathan smiled. "It wouldn't be that bad in a long-sleeved wetsuit, and I can look into some topographical maps and bathymetric maps to make sure it's safe."

Brianna raised her eyebrow. "I'm not sure exactly what you're over there planning, but I like the idea of you taking me on a relaxing vacation to the Caribbean and teaching me to scuba dive around coral reefs or something. The water out here does not look tempting at all."

Brianna walked toward the door. "I'm going to go check on Jenna and grab a snack, do you want anything?

Nathan shook his head, "No, you go ahead, but I would like to talk more about this when you come back. Some plans are starting to come together too perfectly for coincidence."

She smiled. "Sure. Give me an hour and I'll be back." She left and went to check on Jenna. First, she looked for her in her "trap room." The little girl had taken to spending hours in there playing every day. She'd covered the room in string and caltrops made from pointy pieces of cardboard.

"Jenna! Are you in here? We aren't playing hide-and-seek right now." She got no response, but that didn't mean she wasn't hiding. Brianna watched her step. After ten minutes of carefully ducking under string and crawling around obstacles to look under every piece of furniture, she decided Jenna really wasn't there.

At the rate this girl is going, soon I won't be able to enter this room at all. This isn't exactly what I meant when I promised she could make whatever traps she wanted in here. Hopefully, this is the last time I underestimate a Riley.

Brianna checked the kitchen. Jenna wasn't there. She had an uncomfortable memory of losing Jenna before when she first became her governess on Riley's Paradise Island. More swiftly, she moved from room to room, searching for Jenna. She couldn't find her in the main part of the restored castle. *Looks like it is time to search the off-limits parts. Someone's going to be in a lot of trouble.*

Brianna headed to the west wing but didn't have to go very far. Relief washed over her as she spotted the little girl. Then curiosity grabbed her thoughts as she tried to figure out what Jenna was doing.

Jenna was lying on the ground on the restored side of the caution tape. She had a small bowl of chicken beside her, and one arm stretched under the caution tape with a small piece of chicken in her hand. A calico cat sat just out of reach, watching the chicken intently. Every once in a while, she let out a meow until she finally took a piece of chicken from Jenna's fingers and ran back down the hall.

"Jenna! There you are! I was looking all over for you!"

Jenna stood up. "I stayed on the safe side of the caution tape. I did. I listened."

"Jenna, look down. It looks like you made a new friend." Brianna pointed at Jenna's feet. The cat sat next to the bowl, swiftly chomping down on the last of the chicken.

"Yeah," Jenna simply answered, "but she won't let me pet her. Can I keep one of her kittens?"

Brianna frowned. "I'm sorry, sweetheart, but the kittens are too young to leave their mother yet. They are so little that they're just learning how to open their eyes, and they need their mommy's milk to eat."

"Please! I want a pet of my very own. I'll feed the kitten, and she can sleep in my room."

Brianna sighed. "I'll talk to your dad about getting you a pet when we get home, but I'm not sure it would be a good idea to take on that kind of responsibility so far from home. When we get back to our island, why don't you help me more with Chee Chee? We can start practicing for when you get a pet of your own."

Jenna nodded but pouted.

Brianna picked up the empty bowl as they walked back to the main living areas. "You can pick a name for the mom cat. Then we will let Hector know she's here to make sure she gets taken care of. We'll ask if he can help us find good homes for the mom and her babies."

Jenna perked up. "I want to name her Brownie because I thought she was a brownie causing mischief in the castle."

Brianna smiled. "I think that's the perfect name for her."

Brianna and Jenna made their way to the drawing room. As soon as they entered, Nathan turned to them with a big, successful smile on his face. "Jenna, I hired a new friend to babysit you from a highly recommended business in the local town of Tober. She is on her way to Dunam Castle now."

Jenna jumped up and down and yelled, "Yippee! I'm going to make her a welcome card!" Then, like a whirlwind, she ran out of the room.

Nathan cleared his throat, making Brianna turn toward him. "Brianna, I listened to every word you said, and while I understand Scotland isn't as colorful as a coral reef, we actually have snorkeling lessons starting in a few hours."

Brianna stared at Nathan. "Nathan, I thought we talked about this. You can't just decide for me and spring it on me. You need to ask me. This relationship can't work that way anymore. I'm not your employee that you can just tell what to do."

Nathan looked at her sheepishly. "I'm sorry, Brianna. I had already booked it before you expressed your misgivings. I just got so excited that everything worked out with just a few phone calls." Nathan's voice pleaded as he looked at her with his brows arched upwards. "Please come with me? All I'm asking right now is for you to learn to snorkel in a swimming pool. The instructors will go over all the equipment and wetsuit so that you understand exactly how everything works. Then we will jump into an in-ground pool that's large for a pool but tiny compared to the ocean. The water will be clear, and the instructors will be right there, walking you through every step of the way. If you really don't want to, I'll just call them back and cancel."

Brianna was a bit mollified that Nathan finally asked instead of demanding her attendance. A swimming pool didn't sound too scary. They really could use a bit of time alone together. She loved Jenna dearly, but this was supposed to be their honeymoon. In fact, she kind of felt that Nathan had become so wrapped up in this treasure hunt that he had completely forgotten what a romantic getaway for two was supposed to look like. Usually, they didn't include training in cold, murky water.

Brianna took a deep breath. "Okay, I will learn to snorkel in a pool with you. Just to be clear, I am not agreeing to go into the murky, rocky, Scottish sea. Is that a deal?" Nathan nodded. He seemed suspiciously satisfied with that compromise. Nathan and Brianna shook hands, and Brianna went to get ready for her lesson.

After a long few hours of learning everything there was to know about snorkeling, Brianna was exhausted. Nathan joined her in the lessons, even though he had more snorkeling and scuba diving experience than the teacher. She appreciated the gesture.

They walked in the front door and Brianna spotted red powder all over the floor outside the drawing room.

"Aha!" Nathan exclaimed. "Someone set off my trap! I made sure Jenna and the babysitter knew that the room was off-limits. Now all we have to find is the person who has red dye on them that won't come off and we will know who has been sneaking around our castle."

Brianna crossed her arms as she looked at the giant mess. "Are we going to pay to remodel this floor now? If it's water soluble, how do you know your culprit won't just wash off this dye?"

Nathan sent her a dazzling smile. "Don't worry, this powder only stains human skin. It won't leave a mark on anything else. I would suggest that you might want to use gloves when cleaning it off. We don't have to worry about someone washing it off because it stays on the skin for a good week, despite washing. Now we just need to get a peek at the culprit."

Brianna gave Nathan a flat look. "You mean *you* will need to wear gloves when cleaning this up, right?"

Nathan looked at Brianna with a half-grin. "Yes, of course. I'll clean this up. You get some rest. Thank you for coming with me and learning to snorkel."

Brianna found the babysitter reading books with Jenna in her room. Not an ounce of red dye was on either of them. When Jenna spotted her, she squealed, "You're back! We had so much fun baking muffins and cookies tonight!"

Brianna smiled and hugged Jenna. "I missed you. I'm glad you had a delightful time. Just curious, did either of you go into the drawing room and see red dye anywhere? Did you see anyone around?"

The nanny shook her head. *I really should have asked Nathan what her name was.* "No, It was just the two of us. We baked most of the time and did some drawing in the kitchen. Then we came up to Jenna's room to read and start settling down for the night. We didn't see anyone come in, and we didn't go into the drawing room. Is something wrong?"

Brianna shook her head. "Nothing you guys need to worry about. Thank you for taking good care of Jenna. I'll put her to bed. Nathan is downstairs to pay you. Just make sure if you see anything red, don't touch it."

The babysitter said goodbye to Jenna and left. Brianna got the little girl settled into bed, read her a story, and sang her a song before turning out the lights. Exhausted from the long day, she opened her bedroom door, ready to drop into bed. I *guess I should probably take a bath first... What in the world?*

Lying there on top of her bed, Brianna spied Nathan's brother, Jackson. He was sleeping completely naked on top of her bedsheets. A few red splotches of dye on his face, hands, and arms were the only things ruining his otherwise perfect skin. All of his glory hung out, showcased for anyone to see.

Chapter 21

Naked and Unafraid

Brianna

Brianna shouted, "What are you doing in my bed? Why are you naked?"

It startled Jackson out of his slumber, and he jerked upwards into a sitting position with his eyelids still half closed. He had dark shoulder-length hair, a goatee, and a mustache. He was in his mid-twenties, and Brianna was used to seeing him in rather flashy clothing.

He opened his eyes in surprise and unhurriedly moved a pillow down to cover his waist. "Well, hello, Brianna. It looks like I must have fallen asleep. Things at home are so stressful right now, and I was just so tired after the cab dropped me off here. After my shower, when I laid down to air-dry myself, I must have fallen asleep. Sorry for the show. I hope you can still sleep tonight."

A few minutes later, Nathan burst into the room. "I heard shouting. Is everything all right?" His eyes landed on Jackson. "What are you doing naked in my wife's bed?"

Jackson smirked. "Hey, Natey. I'm a bit confused. I saw another room with your things in it. If this is Brianna's room, then there must be some trouble in paradise. Does this mean Brianna is free..."

Before Jackson could say anything more, Nathan picked Jackson's clothes up from the floor and threw them at him. It was all covered in the red dye.

Jackson pulled on his boxers and pants. "Okay, okay. I get the point. You don't appreciate a masterpiece when you see it. Brianna's bathroom had the best-smelling shampoo and soaps, so really, I had no choice but to use her bathroom."

Nathan stared at Jackson, grinding his teeth until Jackson finally got dressed. "What's wrong with you? You should never feel comfortable being naked around my wife. Do you understand me? Why are you here anyway? I'm having a really hard time not breaking your nose right now. You messed up the trap I set."

Jackson frowned and lowered his head and ended up with a petulant look that one might expect from a toddler. "After father abandoned me to be with his new amour, I *thought* you would want your brother safe from the hurricane, but it appears I was mistaken. I should just go back home and get washed away into the sea."

Nathan grabbed his brother's arm and dragged him out of the bedroom. He turned to Brianna. "Why don't you get yourself ready for bed? You look exhausted. I'll get my brother settled."

Brianna nodded but stayed in the hallway. She was too tired to deal with Jackson, but she wanted to know what was going on with their island home. What did Jackson mean about it being swept away?

Nathan turned to Jackson. His tone was short, and Jackson let himself get tugged along. "You, come with me. *Your* room is this way."

"Why are you taking me all the way down the hallway? You don't have to keep me so far from your woman. You can trust me. Can I borrow a change of clothes? I seem to have gotten this outfit all messy."

Nathan stopped in front of the last door in the hallway. "This room is yours. Stay here. I need to find out what's going on at home, and you're getting on my nerves right now."

Nathan turned and stalked down the hallway. When he passed Brianna, he briefly paused. "I'm going to call Dugan. I'll let you know what I find out."

Jackson opened the door he stood in front of and looked around. Brianna smiled to herself as she watched him look into the room and then look back down the hallway at her with his eyebrows raised. "What happened in here? Does a yarn-spinning spider live in here?"

Brianna chuckled. However frustrating Jackson could be, he could still make her laugh. "That's Jenna's trap room. It looks like she's already carrying on the Riley tradition. Right now, she's trying to catch a mythical creature in there."

As if she knew she was being talked about, Jenna came barreling down the hallway in her pajamas as fast as her little legs could carry her. "Uncle Jack! Uncle Jack!" She ran into Jackson at full force. Jackson picked her up and swung her around. She gave him a big hug. "I've missed you so much. I thought I heard your voice and was so excited that I just *had* to get out of bed and see you. When did you get here? Why are you all red?"

Jackson smiled and gave Jenna a kiss on the forehead. "I missed you too, little one. It was my hope that I could surprise you when I got here an hour or two ago, but I didn't see anyone. I accidentally set off your daddy's trap that turned most of me red. I tried to clean it off but wasn't very successful. At least your beds here are comfortable."

However eccentric, Brianna had to admit that Jackson was wonderful with kids. Maybe it was because he was still a big kid himself. Instead of floating through life, what he needed was a purpose or goal to turn him into an adult. Maybe a good woman would come along and nudge him past this stage of extended adolescence.

Brianna watched as Jackson pointed to the room that had become her "trap room." "It looks like you have been busy, little one. Very impressive in there. You will have to tell me all about it."

Jenna jumped up and down excitedly. "I have been busy! Uncle Jackson, it's so fun here. You are going to love it! I got to play in the sand and catch starfish and have tea parties and picnics. This room is for catching a brownie." Jenna changed the cadence of her voice to be very serious. "Not the chocolate brownie, but the tiny man kind of brownie who cleans. Well, actually, Brownie is my cat."

Jackson raised his eyebrow and shook his head. "Well, I see that you've gotten better at riddles too." He contemplated the room for a few minutes. "Since this is your special room, why don't I move into the one right next to it? That isn't one of your trap rooms too, is it?"

Jenna giggled like he had asked a ridiculous question. "No, silly. Brianna made me move my kitchen trap, hallway trap, and stairway trap all into this one room. She said she needed to cook and stuff."

Jackson nodded. "Yes, I agree. That woman is entirely too sensible. We will have to work on that." Jackson bopped Jenna on the nose. "Can you show me where the kitchen is? I am famished. A good nap certainly makes you hungry."

Jenna held Jackson's hand as she led him quietly downstairs, and Brianna followed, considering if she wanted a late snack too. In the kitchen, Jackson stuck his head in the fridge. "Do you think there is any chicken or steak in here? Meat is the best nighttime snack."

Jenna shrugged. "I don't know. I fed most of it to my cat."

Jackson frowned. "Lucky cat."

Jackson fished around in the fridge and freezer to find them something to share. Brianna yawned and went into her room to get herself cleaned up for bed. She was too tired to eat. She needed to get Jenna back to bed soon so she wasn't too cranky tomorrow, but also wanted to give her a bit of time with the uncle she missed horribly.

Roughly ten minutes later, Brianna came into the kitchen and caught the two of them having an ice cream snack. "Jackson, did you guys really need ice cream? With all that sugar in Jenna's system, she'll never go to bed."

Both Jackson and Jenna gave mirroring grimaces, acknowledging their guilt. Jackson said, "I tried to eat vegetables for our snack, but Jenna was a bad influence and made me eat ice cream." Jenna's eyes narrowed at him, and she pursed her lips.

Brianna rolled her eyes and gave a loud sigh. "Come on, *children*. Finish up your snack and then it's back to bed."

Chapter 22

Stormy Romance

Nathan

Nathan was so angry his whole body shook. He took a few deep breaths. Dugan was only a call away, but he was too upset to talk yet. He paced back and forth in the drawing room, clenching and unclenching his fists. He couldn't remember a time when he was this furious with Jackson.

When would he grow up? His brother just showed up out of nowhere thinking it was perfectly acceptable to be naked on his wife's bed? Then he off-handedly mentioned a big storm without giving him any details, like life was some kind of big joke.

While he loved his brother, it was just like him to be unreliable, immature, uninformative... he could go on and on all night naming Jackson's many faults. His nerves were shot. *I should just kick him out. Let him go find some Highland cattle to cuddle up with tonight.*

It was tempting, but he knew it would probably backfire. Jackson had a way of worming his way into the hearts of the women around him. If Nathan kicked him out, it would devastate Jenna. Despite his many faults, Brianna felt Jackson was harmless and humorous. *I just know I would end up the bad guy in that situation. Sometimes I just want to strangle him!*

Nathan's pacing slowed down, and he picked up a cup of lukewarm tea from earlier in the day and chugged the remaining few mouthfuls of liquid. He had business to deal with. He didn't have the luxury of letting his emotions run away with him.

He was ready to call Dugan and get some answers. He needed to know what was going on at home. What he really wanted to know was why his right-hand man hadn't already called him to keep him in the loop.

Nathan dialed Dugan's number. His stomach felt like it was bunched up in knots. Luckily, Dugan answered after only a few rings. "I am so happy to hear from you! I have been running around like a chicken with his head cut off and trying to reach you all day, sir. Unfortunately, cell service has been spotty around these parts as of late, and I've been too busy taking care of things to drive to the mainland yet."

Nathan smiled at hearing his head of security's odd sayings. That calmed him down enough to jump right to the point. "Dugan, what's going on? Jackson is here, and he said something about a storm."

"Yes, as soon as they announced a hurricane was coming through, he dropped off his horse with me and went running. I'm surprised he's already there. They announced the storm last night, and he must have caught a plane sometime this morning to be in Scotland already."

Nathan nodded. "Give me a full status report so I know what we're dealing with."

Dugan went into reporting mode and got to the point as much as Dugan was capable of. "The weathermen are predicting this storm to be one of the worst that's come through here in decades, and it's scheduled to hit the area in the next four or five days. Currently, I am evacuating all the animals like Noah and the ark. Luckily, Thomas, that man you hired to help with your hobby farm, has taken it as his personal duty to protect your farm critters."

"Where are you two taking the animals?"

Dugan answered, "Thomas rented a ferry that is specifically designed for moving livestock. We made arrangements to rent some space from a farm not too far off the coast a few hours north of Riley's Paradise Island. It's been a lot of work today, but we almost have everyone there now."

Nathan pursed his lips. "What happened with the construction crew and staff you were hiring? Aren't they supposed to be starting soon so that everything would run smoothly by the time we get home?"

Dugan answered slowly, after a brief pause. "Like a pup with his tail between his legs, I hate to tell you this, sir, but we had to postpone construction on the new staff housing indefinitely. All the staff I hired have been called and put on hold until we find out what kind of damage we are dealing with. Thomas got a hold of everyone from the phone lines on the mainland except for one woman, but I'm sure I will be able to contact her before the storm comes."

"It is what it is. Make sure you get a hold of that last woman. I don't want anyone on that island until it's safe again. A minor storm creates chaos with all of those traps. I can't imagine what will happen after this one."

"I will make it a priority to contact her, sir." More slowly, he added, "I'm sorry, sir. I couldn't get a hold of you, and I needed to make some quick decisions. We don't have a lot of time, and we don't know what will be left once this storm is finished with us. Once we assess the damage the island sustained, you can let us know how you want us to proceed."

That is about as loquacious as I have ever heard Dugan be. He must really be upset. Nathan reassured him, "Thank you, my good man. You made the right decision under the circumstances. I appreciate that I can trust you to take care of things when I'm gone."

As if he had a sudden afterthought, Dugan quickly said, "Oh, and your father told me to tell you he is staying at Debbie's house. He said they will travel inland as necessary and not to worry about him. I assured Mr. Riley that I would let you know when I talked to you."

Nathan ran his hand through his hair. "Thanks for telling me. This must really be a bad one. I don't remember having to evacuate since I was a boy."

Dugan paused before answering. "Thomas said the entire area is chaos and evacuation centers are already filling up. This is to be the behemoth of storms. They are calling it Hurricane Karen."

Nathan hung up and searched on his phone for the local news around Riley's Paradise Island. All the reports looked pretty bad. Yes, they were having a nice vacation in Scotland, but what if they didn't have a home to go back to when they were done?

Chapter 23

Bacon

Brianna

The next morning, Brianna woke up to the smell of bacon. She followed her nose to the kitchen to see Jackson making eggs, bacon, and lots of pancakes. He turned to her as she walked into the kitchen. Even though he was in fresh clothing, she couldn't help but smile at the red blotches that still covered his face.

"Good morning! I made breakfast to apologize for barging in on your honeymoon. There is a lot of bacon because I know it's Nathan's favorite. I felt he might be a tad angry with me after last night."

Brianna's mouth watered, so she grabbed a plate and started loading it with pancakes. "Thank you. That was very thoughtful of you. Nathan came and told me about the hurricane coming through. I could hardly sleep a wink last night. How bad is it at home?"

Jackson's smile faltered. "I know I joke, but you really should brace yourself. Storms always hit our island worse than the mainland, and this is going to be a bad one. We may not be going home for a good while."

Nathan cleared his throat from behind them. Brianna and Jackson both turned to see him watching them with an eyebrow raised. "Am I interrupting something?"

Brianna gave Nathan a smile and walked over to give him a quick kiss while balancing her overflowing plate. "Your brother was nice enough to cook us breakfast. He even made you bacon." She stared at him for an awkwardly long time, waiting for Nathan to say something nice in return. When he said nothing, she raised an eyebrow and nodded her head toward Jackson to give him a nudge.

Nathan let out a gigantic sigh. "Thank you for making us breakfast, Jackson. You always have a place with us if there is a problem, but please, in the future, call first."

Jackson filled a plate to the brim with only bacon and handed it to Nathan. "You've got it, bro. I knew you would have my back."

Nathan looked at his plate of bacon and rolled his eyes. Jackson got out a second plate to add eggs and a pancake too, but still filled up the other half of his plate with an abnormally gigantic pile of bacon. He sat down next to Brianna, pulling his chair extra close to her.

A few minutes later, Jenna came charging into the kitchen. "Uncle Jackson! You're still here! I was afraid it was a dream!"

Jackson chuckled. "No, little one. It wasn't a dream. We really ate ice cream together in the middle of the night. If you're still hungry, I made a pancake especially for you. It's shaped like a tiny man with a broom, just like you described the brownie to be."

After plating the pancake, he handed it to Jenna. She held the plate, studying it for a minute. "That doesn't look like a little man. It looks like a blob."

Raising an eyebrow at her, Jackson said, "Then I guess you will have to teach me how to make him better next time. Hopefully, your blob at least tastes good."

Jenna took her plate to the table, covered her pancake in a lake of syrup, and took a bite. "Mmmm... he is tasty." Between bites, she looked up at Nathan. "Daddy, what are we doing today?"

Nathan looked over at Brianna. "Well, if Brianna wants to, I thought maybe we could check out the Folklore Festival that starts up today. It runs all week, but I could really use a distraction today."

An enormous smile grew across Brianna's face. "That sounds like fun. Let's do it. I think that's exactly what our little family needs today."

Nathan held up a finger. "Well, there is a catch. Everyone who attends this festival usually wears a costume of some sort, themed after the local folklore or mystical creatures. Do you think we could pull something together that fast?"

Jenna said, "I want to be a brownie! No, a fairy. Maybe a mermaid. Can I be a dragon?"

Brianna chuckled. "I'm not sure we will have the most elaborate costumes, but I think I can pull something together for each of us if you give me an hour or two. If we can narrow down what we are going as."

Nathan nodded. "I have an idea for my costume, so you don't have to worry about me, but I have a project I want to get ready before we leave. I think I figured out a foolproof way to know who is snooping around our castle. Do you think we can be ready to leave by eleven? I'm sure there will be plenty of fair food that we can pick something up for lunch while we're there."

Brianna gave Nathan a kiss on the cheek. "Yes, we will be ready. I'm really looking forward to having a nice, relaxing day with you. Sometimes it's nice to do something purely recreational with no ulterior motives." Nathan gave her a funny look but stayed quiet.

As they cleaned up their plates, Jenna said, "I could wear a sword and be a knight, or I could bring lots of chocolate brownies and eat them and be a brownie monster..."

Jackson finished cooking, filled his plate up with food, and walked past them to sit at the table. "I have the perfect costume in mind. Don't worry, I'll be ready to go at eleven too."

Nathan turned to leave, but Brianna caught sight of him rolling his eyes. At least they weren't arguing anymore.

Chapter 24

How Medieval

Brianna

Brianna watched as Jenna looked around excitedly at all the stands and people dressed up at the festival. She wore a sparkling dress with wings and a flowery headband. They'd pinned a tiny fake bird in her hair.

She waved her magic wand around. "Uncle Jack, I am going to turn you into a toad!" Brianna had dressed her up as a fairy. They'd covered her costume in more glitter and fake gems than the other attendants at the Scottish folklore festival, but it was what she wanted, so Brianna had helped her make the costume from some of the dress-up clothes they had brought with them.

Jackson wore a suit with a mask that resembled a red fox more than a wolf. It was his artistic interpretation of what a wulver should look like. It cleverly covered most of the red dye that still stained his face. When Jenna pointed the wand at him, he clutched his chest and dramatically fell to his hands and knees. "Oh, no! The fairy got me! I will forever belong to the fairy folk now!"

Brianna was looking at a stand that had small decorative boxes that reminded her of the box Nathan had used when he proposed to her on their paradise island. She even found one that had a secret compartment.

Jackson hopped around between a jewelry stand and a pottery stand. A child pointed, and a crowd gathered around him. They seemed to believe that he was part of the paid entertainment. Forever the ham, Jackson frolicked on all fours, making a ribbit sound until a loud ripping sound stopped him mid-hop. The crowd roared with laughter. Jackson stood up and looked at his behind until he spotted a large tear. Seemingly unperturbed, he bowed until, eventually, the people dispersed.

Jackson walked over to Brianna, looking truly sheepish for the first time since she had met him. Jenna stood with her and used a hand to pet the soft fur on the cape of her costume. Brianna wore a black bathing suit with black stretch pants and had cut a gray blanket to be a pretend seal skin draped around her. She had come as a selkie.

Jackson fluttered his eyes at Brianna. "Darling, I appear to have a problem with my bottom. Do you think you could help a poor man out? I will be as still as a statue if you wouldn't mind sewing me up."

Brianna rolled her eyes and dug into her purse. "I brought a needle and some thread for Jenna's costume. As long as you don't mind it being bright pink, it should at least temporarily hold your pants together until we get home."

She handed him the needle and thread and batted her own eyes at him. "Being that you are such an intelligent man, I'm sure you can figure out how to sew up your own pants." Brianna pointed toward the pottery stand. "I saw a sign for bathrooms pointing that way. I have faith that you can figure it out."

Brianna picked up Jenna's hand and looked around. Where had Nathan gone? He had mentioned something about falconry. A man painted green and a woman covered in fur walked past. It was really hard to pick people out with all the costumes.

Over there! Brianna spotted a stand that held a hawk and an owl standing on large sticks with little hoods over their faces. Brianna held

Jenna's hand tightly as she crossed through a row of stands to see if Nathan was there.

When they neared the stand, they saw Nathan with dirt smudged on his face and dressed in rags. He held an old-fashioned straw broom in his hand. He was talking to a practically naked woman. Jenna ran to the brownie and hugged his legs.

The woman turned and narrowed her eyes at Brianna. Brianna realized who Nathan was talking to. Anger and jealousy took over her normally calm demeanor. After giving Florine a small false smile and nodding her head in greeting, she stood to talk to Nathan with her back to the woman.

She wore a small black strip of fabric over her breasts and a bikini thong for a bottom. Her high-heeled shoes were covered with fabric to make them look like hooves. The brownie that was Nathan looked away from Florine to return Jenna's hug and turned to talk to Brianna.

Unashamedly, Jenna whispered loudly, "Daddy, doesn't that lady know you're supposed to wear clothes when you're outside?"

Florine's nasal voice answered Jenna. "Jenna, it's me, Florine. For the folklore festival, I'm dressed as a kelpie. I miss you, little one. I haven't seen you in so long, but your father tells me that your uncle is staying with you guys and will watch you now. Convince your daddy that I should come over and play again." She stuck her lip out in a pout.

Jenna spotted the birds, and they directed her focus to a new stand. "Look, Daddy! They brought birds to the Scottish folklore fair! Can I pet one?"

Sometimes Brianna was glad that the little girl was so easily distracted.

Florine slipped away, and Brianna watched as the woman tripped on her high heels, causing her to bump into a man wearing a robe and a wizard's hat. *Would Merlin turn her into a toad, perhaps?*

Brianna turned to see Nathan kneeling down at eye level with Jenna. "These birds aren't wild, but they are also not pets. These are hunting birds that would bite you if you tried to pet them."

"Why are they wearing little hats that cover their eyes?" Jenna inquired.

Despite all the commotion going on around them, Nathan's full attention focused on his own Little Bird. "All the people here at the fair would make the birds nervous if they could see. The hats keep the birds calm. Don't worry. Do you see that trailer behind his stand? The man who owns them said that he sometimes puts the birds in there if they get too stressed from the crowds."

Jenna peppered Nathan with more questions. "Why would they bring the birds to the festival if it would scare them?"

Brianna admired Nathan's calm patience. She leaned closer because she was also curious to hear his response. "Well, the birds are here for a few reasons. Do you see that gentleman over there? His name is Jasper."

Nathan pointed out a tall, muscular yet trim man not dressed as a creature of folklore but wearing a traditional kilt with a scabbard hanging from it. "The birds attract people to come to his stand to buy some of the falconry supplies he brought. He likes the sport of falconry and wants to tell people about it."

Nathan pointed to a few pamphlets about rehabilitating birds of prey. "These birds are also ones that he rehabilitated. He is trying to gain awareness about how he saves and trains the birds. He even gave me one of his cards. If we ever see an injured bird of prey, all we need to do is call him."

Looking around, Brianna zoned out and remembered her times selling her glass animal figurines that she loved to make. She felt a longing to be on the other side of those craft tables.

She really missed selling her glass animals at fairs and festivals. She enjoyed showing off her art and teaching people about how she made her little creations, and she even missed doing live demonstrations. Wide-eyed children and adults alike would watch her, mesmerized, as she worked.

She would have to sign up as a vendor for a craft festival in the fall. Brianna had packed her equipment but hadn't gotten it out once since she'd married Nathan.

Have I lost myself?

Maybe that was part of her frustration with Nathan. She was living his life instead of blending both of theirs together. She would have to work on that. When they got home, she would start working on her backlog of inventory to sell. Brianna felt giddy with anticipation at her upcoming plans.

A horn blew, and a man wearing a bloody torn shirt walked through the venues. A bogle, perhaps? "All lords and ladies are invited to see our champion fight the mighty beihir. Venture forth to the field!" He repeated his message roughly every twenty feet.

The crowd left the venues and streamed toward the field. Nathan paused at a food stand to pick up a few turkey legs. Then Nathan, Jenna, and Brianna followed the crowd.

When they arrived at the field, Jackson waved them down. Somehow, he had charmed his way into a spot on a hill that had a magnificent view and was shaded by the trees behind them. He was thoughtful enough to save them seats. Sometimes having a megalomaniac for a brother-in-law had its benefits.

Brianna noted the bright pink strip of thread that inexpertly wormed its way down the back of Jackson's pants. It stuck out like a sore thumb on his suit, but Jackson didn't seem to notice or care. They all settled down on the grass when a trumpet announced the beginning of the show.

A few actors went out into the field and mimed doing everyday tasks. One seemed to build something, one was chopping firewood, and one was cooking over a fire. Suddenly, a giant snake-like dragon burst into the field from a blue shimmering tunnel. The head part was held up by one person and the body was held up by three more people. The creature took a few laps of the field, showing off its magnificence.

The person in front would move in one direction and then the people directly behind them would follow with a slight delay. This created an undulating motion that seemed very serpentine. The great beihir ran by each of the common people in the field, and they all fell over, presumably dead.

The field cleared, and the beihir returned to the blue tunnel. A man dressed in a traditional kilt wooed a woman. They danced about on the field happily together until the beihir made another appearance. The man drew his sword and stepped in front of the woman to protect her. A liquid shot from the beihir and hit the man, making him dramatically clutch at his chest and fall over.

The beihir took off around the field to prance in victory as the woman knelt beside her love in anguish. The woman looked up at the beihir with determination and ran toward its blue, watery home. After noticing her sprint, the beihir made a struggle to beat her there. It didn't move extremely fast, but it still impressed Brianna that one of the men holding up its body didn't trip and fall over his own feet.

Both the woman and the beihir were neck and neck by the time they made it to the tunnel. In order to get ahead, the woman dove into the tunnel and disappeared. The beihir soon followed. Everything was still for a few moments. The audience was completely silent, even Jenna. Eventually, the man in the middle of the field slowly rose.

He felt his body all over, as if in shock that he was truly alive, and then dramatically looked around for the woman. Realizing that she was lost, he clutched his heart and dropped to the ground on his knees, his head hung low.

After a moment, he picked up his sword and pointed it at the sky. He took off at a run toward the tunnel and charged inside, sword first. He came back out a moment later carrying his sword in one hand and the creature's head in the other. The hero had avenged his love's sacrifice.

A few people dressed as monsters of folklore entered the field. Florine flounced around in her outfit, showing off every exposed curve. The hero traveled through the field. Each creature tried to fight or entice him. He fought them all and overcame every challenge but remained forever alone.

Nathan smiled sadly at Brianna, feeling the emotions of the drama in front of them. Jenna yawned, and suddenly, a smile spread across Nathan's face. "Jenna's tired. Let's work our way back to the castle. That should have been enough time to catch a changeling in my trap."

Brianna gave an exaggerated sigh while a smile played upon her lips. "Why did I decide I wanted to be a Riley again?"

Chapter 25

Changeling Trap

Brianna

Brianna held Jenna's hand and followed Nathan through the crowd of mythological creatures and legends. After a while of Jenna lagging, Nathan picked her up and stuck her on his shoulders. They zigzagged past a giant man with one eye painted on his forehead and walking on stilts.

Jackson was walking along with them until his eyes caught on a beautiful woman dressed in an almost sheer gown and sporting a sword. "You guys go on ahead. I'll find my own ride back to the castle." Then he took off and was soon lost in the crowd. *There is no lack of confidence in that man.*

A young woman dressed in an elaborate sparkling fairy costume blew bubbles at Jenna. Jenna squealed in excitement. "She's dressed like me! Maybe we should pretend that she is my older sister."

An older woman at one stand was yelling about her food cart. "Come, ye! Come, ye! The tasty haggis may be extinct, but our special recipe replicates the taste and texture of the original!" Brianna blanched at the thought of eating sheep innards and looked away. She felt like she was going to be sick.

Brianna quickly glanced at stands filled with medieval trinkets, fantasy books, and pre-sewn costumes for sale. There was still so much that they hadn't seen, but for now, they were done shopping. Nathan's goal was to get back to the castle and check on his latest trap, and

Brianna's fingers were itching to make a few glass animals inspired by their time in Scotland. She thought she would start with a seal.

Nathan stopped abruptly in front of a blacksmith stand. Brianna had to stop just as quickly behind Nathan. This caused a man dressed as a large green serpent to bump into her. He shook his head at her as she tried to say, "Sorry!"

His eyes not leaving the stand, Nathan watched a man dressed in a leather apron hammer at a strip of iron. He had thick gloves on and was bending the iron into a hook using long, red-hot metal tools. *Interesting. The way he forms the metal reminds me of how I form glass into shapes. Very different mediums, but I can see the artistic side of blacksmithing.*

Jenna leaned down from Nathan's shoulders so she could see better. The blacksmith used a clamp to pick up the newly formed hook, and he placed it back in the small forge that he had set up in his stand. When he took it out of the coals, it was bright red again from the heat.

He twisted the malleable iron and punched a hole into it. Finishing his art, he used the clamp to hold the hot hook in a bucket of water. Steam billowed from the bucket.

Something looked familiar about the man. He looked out of place dressed as a blacksmith and a little rounder in the face. Behind all the soot, Brianna realized it was Lewis, the man who had lent her the coat at Beihir's Pub. The man who had helped them decipher their first clue in Captain Kiddle's treasure map.

No wonder he was so familiar with Scottish folklore. He was a major attraction at the local Folklore Festival. This also explained why he was so interested in getting a closer look at the swords that decorated the walls of the drawing room back at the castle. It was professional interest because he was a blacksmith!

The blacksmith finished his hook, set down his tools, and wiped the sweat from his brow. He took off his leather apron and gloves. Then he moved to stand in front of his stand where, presumably, the heat was a little less intense. He spotted Nathan and held out a sooty hand, dirty despite the gloves.

He smiled as he spoke. "Welcome to my humble smithy. How kind of you magical creatures to mingle amongst us common folk."

Nathan smiled. "Interesting hobby you have here. We enjoyed the blacksmith demonstration, and I wanted to thank you for your tips on our map. We didn't find much, but we have been making progress. Thank you for getting us started in the right direction."

Raising an eyebrow, he shook his head. "I know not of what you speak, but a map leads to only one thing." It impressed Brianna how dedicated Lewis was to the role of his character, or maybe he was just shy about the fight she and Nathan had after he helped them with the map.

"Treasure?" Jenna asked.

"A map leads to where you've been or where you're going!" The blacksmith chortled at his own joke. Lewis was a lot jollier than when they met him last, but maybe that was just the character he was playing.

He winked at Jenna. "Look at this wee fairy. Would you spare me from your beguiling magic for a gift?"

Jenna giggled and nodded. The blacksmith walked over to his stand and picked up a small bracelet made of chain mail. He knelt and presented the gift to Jenna. "A gift for the fair folk. I would not dare risk your ire with a gift of iron."

Jenna placed the thin bracelet on her wrist and turned it back and forth, admiring it. "Thank you so much! I love it!"

Brianna smiled at him. "Thank you. You are always so kind."

He cocked his head and studied Brianna but didn't respond.

Nathan bought an iron hook similar to the one they watched him make during his demonstration and handed it to Jenna. Then he ushered Brianna and Jenna on toward the exit.

Pleased with their afternoon at the festival, the three of them finally made it back to their car. Jenna fell asleep almost immediately. Nathan sped down the country lane, humming with excitement. Hopefully, they would soon know who was breaking into the drawing room.

They passed Hector on a tractor, cutting the high grass on the castle grounds. They waved at him, and he waved back at them as they drove on.

When they were in sight of the castle, Nathan turned to Brianna. "Want to make a bet?"

Brianna raised her eyebrow, interest piqued. "What exactly do you have in mind?"

Nathan smiled mischievously. "I bet that the person who has been stealing things from the drawing room is Hector. If I'm right, move back into the bedroom with me."

Brianna considered this offer. Had they worked through their issues? They still had work to do, but so did any marriage. Maybe it was time to move on. She missed her nights with him.

Regardless, Brianna's stubborn streak played devil's advocate. "All right, I'll take that bet. I think the person who has been sneaking into the castle is Florine."

Nathan frowned. "It can't be Florine. We saw her at the festival today."

Brianna crossed her arms. "Did you really keep your eye on her the whole time we were at the fair? We were there for hours!"

Nathan continued to frown but didn't respond.

Brianna leaned her head onto Nathan's shoulder while he was driving. "Anyway, if I am right, make me breakfast in bed tomorrow and move into my room."

Nathan smiled at her. "You have a deal!" He held out his hand and shook hers before she could say another word. She felt warm inside with the realization that he didn't seem to mind where he slept as long as it was with her. Maybe they could mend this marriage after all.

Brianna ruminated on why someone was keeping tabs on their treasure hunt. Did they want the treasure for themselves? *Maybe once we find out who is causing the mischief, we will be able to retrieve Nathan's stolen journal and coins.* Hopefully, they would know who was stealing from them soon. *The question is, what do we do about them? Would the police think this was some kind of treasure-hunting joke?*

When they got back to the castle, Nathan carried Jenna in. Brianna waited impatiently at the bottom of the stairs. They agreed to check on the drawing room together. Nathan led the way. The room was a mess. Someone had ransacked it while they were out.

Chapter 26

Nanny Cam

Brianna

Still dressed in her costume, Brianna walked around the room in shock. Papers were scattered across the room and furniture lay overturned. One sword on the wall was even missing. She knelt down to the floor and gingerly picked up Nathan's book, *Monstrosities of Scotland*. Some pages were bent, but at least this book was otherwise unharmed.

She smoothed the pages back into place. She looked around at some of the other books lying on the floor. Someone had haphazardly threw them all over. *Hopefully, Nathan can fix up some of the crumpled and ripped pages, or maybe he can pay someone to fix them.*

Nathan knelt over and picked up the pieces of a broken camera off the ground. "Looks like they took the memory card. We got nothing."

Brianna frowned. "You should have used a more up-to-date camera that provided a live feed. Then you could have seen whoever was doing this before they found the camera."

Nathan shrugged. "They had few options when I went to the local store this morning. If I had planned this out earlier, I could have had one shipped, but I really thought I would hide it well enough that no one would find it."

He ran his hand through his hair as he looked around the room. "I expected something to go missing. So far, something has been out of place or gone almost every time we leave for a full-day adventure.

I'm just surprised at the extent of damage that was wrought this time. I wasn't expecting this. Before, it was very subtle when they stole something."

Brianna pursed her lips. "Hmm... It's almost like someone was in a real hurry to find everything. Maybe because they headed to a festival too..."

Nathan shrugged. "Or maybe they saw our car driving past their cottage and took advantage of an empty castle." Nathan was sure suspicious of Hector. He walked over to the garbage can and threw away the pieces of the camera. Brianna helped him tidy up. They worked together to right an ottoman, and Brianna picked up a few more books to place on the main table of the room.

She gasped. "Nathan, the map! All our notes and clues. It's gone!" The table that once held an enlarged copy of the map, with close-ups of each mysterious riddle and symbol, was missing. A few random pages of notes lay scattered across the table, but it looked like the present-day map of the area was gone as well.

Nathan frowned. "If I had realized that our culprit was going to be this destructive and greedy, I wouldn't have bothered with the camera. Maybe we should have hidden all the pieces of research around the castle instead of using it as bait. I could have made a map to find the pieces of the treasure map."

Brianna looked at him and rolled her eyes. "You know that's not how normal people think, right? Usually, it's not a matter of which kind of trap or distraction would be best. When someone steals something, it's time to call in the police."

Nathan called the police as Brianna went upstairs to get changed out of her selkie outfit. She wanted to check on Jenna. The way the intruder was so fearless about coming in here and destroying the place was making the hair on the back of her neck stand up. Maybe she should move Jenna into her room.

With Brianna's home and privacy being invaded, this treasure hunt was becoming a lot more than just a fun pastime during their honeymoon. She couldn't let whoever was doing this get away with it. They had to find the treasure now, before this thief could.

Slowly, Brianna opened Jenna's bedroom door to find the little girl slumbering peacefully. She walked over and gave her a kiss on the forehead. No matter how crazy things got with this treasure map, the most important treasure of all was lying right there in front of her. Were things getting too dangerous here? They could just pack up and leave, but where would they go when their home was about to be destroyed by a hurricane?

Brianna went into her own room and breathed a sigh of relief that everything looked untouched. Before she built Jenna a bed of blankets on the couch in her room, she needed to check on one more thing. *I just need to put my hands on the original copy of the map to reassure myself that it is still safe.*

Brianna pulled her luggage out from under her bed. She sorted through the extra clothing in there until she came to a copy of the book *Dr. Doolittle* that Jenna and Nathan had gotten her as a wedding gift.

She turned the book and opened the secret compartment. At first, she didn't know what to do with a book that she didn't read but loved it because of who it came from. Only recently she realized it had a practical purpose too. She extracted a small key. *Maybe this crazy family is rubbing off on me.* A small smile played on her lips. She liked the sound of that. *My* crazy family.

She took the key down to the kitchen. She glanced at the kitchen table to see the copy of the map she sometimes looked over while relaxing with a cup of coffee. *Looks like they missed one copy. All is not lost.* She picked it up for safekeeping.

She went into the kitchen pantry and shut the door behind her. Nathan had gotten a safe installed behind the pantry door after they realized things were being stolen. He had tried to get a hold of his aunt, who owned the castle, to ask permission before installing it. Unfortunately, he hadn't been able to reach her since their arrival.

Nathan was getting really concerned. His aunt, Priscilla Riley, had no children of her own, and the police hadn't been very helpful. They reassured him they visited her and she was all right, but they weren't at liberty to discuss anything further. Nathan said maybe he would fly out to California and check on her after their honeymoon. After things calmed down from the hurricane.

Brianna opened the safe and moved Nathan's laptop to the side. She moved the small tin of semiprecious stones and pulled out the old metal tube. Memories of finding it in a cave on Riley's Paradise Island came rushing back to her.

She took it out into the light of the kitchen and gingerly wiggled the wax end loose. Cautiously, she pulled out the original copy of the map and laid it on the table. The ends attempted to curl back in, so she used her arms to hold down the ends as she carefully held the map.

They still had the original, so they could still find the treasure. Although now they were on a timeline. They had to race against an unknown competitor to get to the treasure before them. *It would be a little easier if we knew who we were up against.*

She could see Florine being greedy, and Hector could be creepy, but she honestly wouldn't have marked either of them as a mastermind of puzzles and a treasure hunter that would stop at nothing. There must be a side to one of them they hadn't seen yet.

Brianna re-secured the map and checked in on Nathan. He was making pretty good progress cleaning up the drawing room, and she placed their last copy of the map on the table.

Nathan looked up as she entered the room. "I got a hold of the police. They're going to send someone out to talk with us tomorrow, but they say there isn't a lot they can do with no witnesses or evidence."

After walking over to the copy of the map and gingerly holding it up to the light, Nathan pursed his lips. "A lot of our notes are gone, but at least we aren't starting from scratch. I remember a good deal of what I researched. Besides, we are down to only one last symbol and riddle before uncovering the last bit of treasure. I'll write what I can remember after I finish cleaning up in here."

Brianna nodded and went to get a snack from the kitchen before heading off to bed. The Scottish air sure made her hungry. She heard the front door of the castle creak open and went to investigate.

Jackson placed his key back in his pocket and locked the door behind him. He saw her and gave her a wide Cheshire Cat grin. Cheerfully, he passed her in the hallway, softly whistling to himself as he made his way to his room.

How odd. I have never known that man not to talk about everything. The scent of a woman's perfume drifted in the air behind him, so Brianna decided not to ask questions.

After her snack, Brianna went to her room and got out all of her glass-making supplies. She lovingly took out the small blowtorch and set it beside a handful of colored glass sticks. She took the supplies to the desk in her room and lost herself in creating glass mystical creatures. An hour and a half later, she smiled at the half a dozen creations sitting on the table in front of her. She usually created animals but was feeling inspired by her recent adventures. She thought the mermaid turned out the best.

She left the glass figurines on the table and cleaned up the rest of her supplies, then she turned off the lights. While Jenna was getting heavy, Brianna still picked her up and carried her groggy stepdaughter into the little bed she had made her on the couch in her room. Jenna groaned and clung to her but let herself be moved. She immediately fell back asleep.

I'd better get to sleep. Nathan had scheduled for them to practice snorkeling in the pool some more. She only agreed to snorkeling in a pool, but with how much practice Nathan wanted her to have, she felt like he was just trying to get her comfortable before asking her to go into the ocean with him again. She had to be ready for the police that were coming by to investigate their stolen maps and materials, and they really needed to secure the tunnels she'd found behind that tapestry for their own safety. It was going to be a busy day.

Brianna couldn't fall asleep until Nathan came into her bedroom, braced a chair against the doorknob, and slipped into the bed beside her. It seemed he didn't want them to all be apart either. She tossed and turned and dreamed fitfully of hidden dangers in the castle walls. What seemed like a Scottish paradise now threatened a danger that only time would uncover. Would they end up with treasure or wishing they had just stayed home?

Chapter 27

Secret Passageways

Brianna

The next morning, Brianna checked the batteries in her flashlight, wasting time before entering the secret tunnel. *There are spiders and mice and who knows what else in there.*

Nathan must have seen her hesitation because he put an arm around her shoulder. "I know you found this secret passageway, so I don't want to steal your thunder, but if you're scared, I can go first. What do you want to do?"

As soon as Brianna heard him question if she was scared, she stubbornly set her jaw. *I can do this.* "Of course I'm not scared. I was just checking my flashlight. It's so dark back there, you'll be happy we brought it."

Brianna walked up to the large dusty tapestry. It was rotted with age, but she could still make out a bit of the picture on it. It looked like a detailed portrait of a naked woman sitting on a rock beside a stream. The hanging must have been beautiful at one point in time. What a waste to let it rot here. It surprised her it hadn't fallen down yet.

She pulled the enormous heavy tapestry out from the wall far enough that she could squeeze behind it. Flashlight in front of her, she quickly glanced around before stepping into the darkness. Nathan followed with his own flashlight, bumping into her as she looked around.

A hallway extended to both the right and the left. As her eyes adjusted, she realized that farther down the left hallway were a few pinholes of light shining into the tunnel. She spoke softly to Nathan. "Do you think those lights up there are from the castle deteriorating or purposeful peepholes?"

She felt Nathan shrug directly behind her in the darkness. "We'd better check the bedrooms when we get back, just in case."

Brianna shone her light on the floor. There were the footprints. They disturbed the dust going to the right. "We told Jackson that we would only be gone an hour or two while he watched Jenna. I think we should just follow the footprints. I don't think we're going to have time to explore everything."

She shone the light close enough to Nathan to see his head nod. "Sure, whatever you think." Brianna frowned. He was being suspiciously amicable. Was it because she let him back into her bed, or did he have something else up his sleeve? It wasn't like they could do anything more than sleep in that room with Jenna a few feet away, sleeping on the couch.

Brianna turned to him and pointed the flashlight so she could read his expression without blinding him. "It's killing you not to take over and lead us down this unexplored passageway, isn't it?"

Nathan smiled. "I have been told in the recent past that I sometimes steamroll over people and try to do things my way. It's hard, and I'm not promising that I won't ever do it again, but I am *trying* to let you take the lead more often and be more attentive to your ideas."

Brianna gave him a kiss on the lips and then leaned her forehead on his chest. "I appreciate it a lot. It makes a big difference to me."

Nathan wrapped his arms around her, and Brianna found herself held tight against his chest. She angled her head back up to Nathan's, and he said, "I love you, and I have really missed holding you. I think we need to take another honeymoon after this one that's shorter, but only the two of us."

Leaning down, Nathan placed his hands on either side of her face and gently pressed his lips upon hers. A tingling sensation spread through her body and a fire ignited deep inside her. He was right; it had been too long. Forgetting where they were and what their mission was, their lips came together with a quickly growing ferocity.

She slipped her hands under the brim of Nathan's shirt, wrapped her arms around his back, and pulled him closer. He made a soft sigh as his teeth playfully dragged against her lower lip, and he trailed kisses down her neck. Brianna missed the way this man made her feel, and she dropped her flashlight, forgotten.

A moment after her flashlight hit the ground, Brianna felt a small furry creature run by her leg. With a squeak, she pulled away from Nathan and grabbed for her flashlight. Frantically, she shone the light in all directions, only to see a mouse scurry away from her beam of light.

She gave Nathan a sheepish smile, but the moment was gone, so she turned and followed the footprints. The hallway itself turned and splintered off in different directions several times. It was like a maze. She wondered how the person whose footprints they were following even knew how to get to the tapestry doorway.

At one point, they found two holes at crouching height looking into one of the dilapidated bedrooms. Brianna shivered when she spotted a metal candlestick nearby. The candle had either melted or been eaten away by mice. *This definitely is a peephole.*

Farther down the hallway, they found a narrow area just wide enough to fit a chair. A broken shelf sat next to it, with a few rot-ted-out books and dilapidated toys. "Do you think those were some of Captain Kiddle's things from when he was young? Maybe he hid them here after those horrible people took over his house."

Nathan picked up one book and tried to dust off the cover. The book was moldy and looked like a child's primer. "I don't think we will ever know for sure, unless the owner was nice enough to sign these for us. We can come back to look at these more later."

Nathan set down the books and followed Brianna through a few more twists and turns until they came to a stone stairwell leading downwards. They followed the footprints down into an even darker and mustier tunnel. After they walked a while, Brianna felt something brush against her hair. *Ew, spiderwebs!*

Brianna shone her light toward the ceiling to see roots dangling in the air. They worked their way through the rock above the tunnel and were hanging down into the opening. "We must be outside of the castle now. Do you think there is a minotaur waiting for us in this maze?"

Nathan laughed. "If there is one, I think he has long red hair and extra-long wide horns like the Highland cattle that are all over this countryside."

In the distance, Brianna heard the faint chirping of birds and hope stirred in her chest. After a last turn, they came to a piece of metal that was haphazardly placed in front of a large opening. Light streamed around it where it didn't fully cover the opening. *I wonder if this is how the cat got in.*

They moved the metal and stepped out into a grassy field. It took a few minutes for their eyes to adjust to the bright sunlight. Their tunnel ended at a hill a few yards from a nearby forest.

In front of the opening was a large rock lying in overgrown grass. Nathan went over to investigate it. "Looks like this rock was the original door to these tunnels. It rolled out of the way quite some time ago, though."

Brianna looked around, trying to orient herself. "At least we figured out how the culprit is getting into the castle, but we still have no way of figuring out who did it. Aha, there is the castle." She pointed south of their position. The castle lay about a half-mile away.

Nathan gave her an evil smile. "I know how we can catch our culprit. The next time they sneak into the castle this way, they will be in for a big surprise."

Brianna rolled her eyes. "I've heard that before."

Chapter 28

Mermaids for Breakfast

Brianna

A few days later, there had still been no sign of anyone trying to gain entrance to the castle through the back passageways. Brianna breathed easier but was also waiting for the other shoe to drop.

Nathan led Brianna to the drawing room. He had a bunch of the books he'd recovered from the break-in laid out with post-it notes sticking out of them and numerous note cards laid out on the tables. It looked like the loss of his notebook and a copy of the map hadn't really slowed him down.

Brianna looked at the projector pointing to a large screen and raised her eyebrow. A cozy-looking overstuffed chair with a hot cup of coffee steaming on the end table directly beside it was conveniently positioned in front of the screen. Brianna looked around and caught Nathan in her sights. "This looks more like you're preparing a presentation for a big board meeting than a treasure hunt."

Nathan put his hands on Brianna's shoulders and directed her to sit in the big, overstuffed chair. He stood in front of her and cleared his throat. "To be clear, I, Nathan Riley, am asking and not telling my wife, Brianna Riley, to do something."

Brianna narrowed her eyes at him for his overdramatization, but she was getting nervous about what a big production Nathan was making. *He must want to ask me something life-altering.* Nathan held up his hand. "Please don't say anything yet. At least promise me you won't say no right away. Just let me go through my presentation."

Nathan turned on his laptop and started showing blown-up pictures of the riddle and the symbol of the beihir from the map. "Luckily, I have pictures of a lot of my research on my computer. These are exhibits A and B. They explain why I strongly believe that they hid the treasure on the rock island off the coast."

Nathan changed his pictures to local maps. "I researched the local tides, currents, and topography of the ocean floor. I believe that snorkeling at this location will be perfectly safe. In fact, it is a well-loved pastime of many a Scotsman." Brianna let out the breath that she didn't realize she was holding. All of this was just about snorkeling, nothing more.

Nathan flashed through pictures of whales, fish, and dolphins. "I researched the local marine life and feel we would be safe from predators. If we're lucky, we might see dolphins, seals, sea otters, or a humpback whale. Basking sharks are also more common around here, but although they're large, they are harmless. They eat plankton, not humans."

Nathan got down on one knee and held Brianna's hand. "Brianna, please will you do me the honor of going snorkeling in the Scottish sea with me?"

Brianna couldn't help but laugh. "You laid this on thick, didn't you? While I don't always want you to dictate what we do, you know you just have to ask me. I don't need a big, fancy, dramatic presentation. All I was asking is that you talk to me instead of just making decisions."

Nathan stayed on his knee. "So, is that a yes or a no?"

Brianna rolled her eyes again. It really wasn't too bad in the swimming pool. How much worse could it be in the sea? "Yes, I will go snorkeling with you."

Nathan gave her a hug and a kiss. "You just made me the happiest man in the world."

Brianna looked down at the cold, murky water lapping against the side of the boat. *Next time, I won't let that charming smile get me to say yes.* She glanced over at Nathan calmly driving their boat to the rock island they had explored a few weeks ago.

Her teeth chattered in the wind as she spoke. "I know you said we would anchor the boat safely and it would be fine, but I think I would feel better staying here and guarding the boat."

Nathan glanced over at her, his short hair waving on top of his head from the wind. "If you've changed your mind and feel scared, you don't have to go down with me. Although, if you remember what our instructor said, it's not safe to snorkel alone."

At the word "scared," Brianna's lower jaw set, and she immediately shouted back loudly to be heard over the wind. "I'm not scared. I was just thinking of the boat." Then she crossed her arms and looked at Nathan. Did he just manipulate her on purpose? Activating her stubborn nature and tugging on her need to keep her family safe?

They chugged along in the motorboat for another ten minutes until they reached the island. Brianna squeezed her body into a full-body wetsuit that included gloves and a headpiece to cover her ears. Nathan set the anchor and attached a ladder to the side of the boat so that they could get back in the boat after they were done. He expertly got his suit on and still had time to help Brianna wiggle into the last of her suit.

Brianna stood on the side of the boat, stretching her legs in an attempt to get used to her suit while Nathan got all of their snorkeling equipment out. He handed Brianna her mask, snorkel, fins, and a waterproof flashlight. She couldn't help but giggle as Nathan's feet flapped in his giant flippers as he walked to the edge of the boat. She got out a camera, and she snapped a quick photo of him before stowing it safely back in the boat.

He sat on the side of the boat as it gently rocked in the water. "We're all ready to go. I think you should go first so that I can help you easier if you need it. Just climb down the ladder and breathe through the snorkel, just like we practiced in the pool."

Brianna stood on the boat in her wetsuit, watching the murky water. She must've been insane. Who in their right mind would want to snorkel in that dark, cold water? Next time, she would demand coral reefs!

Before they left, she'd looked up the basking sharks that often swam in these waters. They may not be meat eaters, but they were humongous. Maybe she would be like Jonah and get swallowed by one of those monsters. She sat on the opposite edge of the boat and got her mouthpiece situated. *I can't see down there. I can't do this. I will just have to chicken out.*

Nathan flopped over and knelt in front of her. The weight of them both on the same side of the boat made it tip dangerously. Brianna shouted at him, "Nathan! Go back on your side of the boat! You'll tip us!"

SPLASH! Before Brianna's body could register the shock, she had hit the water. Immediately, she panicked, but then remembered her training. After taking a deep, calming breath, she practiced moving around with her flippers. She looked up to see their boat peacefully floating beside the island and took a deep breath of relief. She really had the worst luck with boats.

She saw a light under the water moving toward her. Soon, Nathan was right up next to her. He patted her down as if checking her over to make sure that she was all right, and then he gave her a thumbs-up under the water. She returned the thumbs-up, and he tapped his flashlight. She switched on her light, so relieved that she didn't drop it.

A shiver ran down Brianna's spine. Her light helped a little in the dark waters, but it also gave her the ability to see just how dark and deep the water was underneath her. *Anything could swim up and eat me, and there is nothing I can do about it. I should have brought a harpoon.* Brianna prayed for courage. She felt like she was swimming in a valley of death.

She shook herself out of her morbid thoughts, and Nathan directed her to follow him over to the rock island. She felt better having something to focus on. They swam all around the side of the rock until Brianna wondered if there was anything here at all, or maybe there was something deeper than they could go. Maybe they should have learned to scuba dive.

Brianna caught sight of Nathan waving his hands. She swam closer, and sure enough, there was a carving on the rock close to the surface of the water. There was a symbol of a beihir that matched the map.

The carving was far larger than the symbols that they had found previously. A few remaining scales showed that the long wingless dragon had originally been intricately carved, but time had washed away the details. The maw of the dragon was still unmistakable. They'd carved large fangs into the rock with a shallow hollow behind them. On closer inspection, Brianna realized that its jaws were clenched around a large silver key.

A key unlocks a treasure chest! It was tarnished, and a few barnacles showed that at some point in time, this part of the rock island had been out of the sea. Nathan took his time as he pried the key out of the beihir's jaws, but despite his efforts, one tooth broke off as he pulled out the key.

Out of the corner of her eye, Brianna caught sight of something dark and fast swimming only a few yards away from her. Her heartbeat sped up. Regardless of how ridiculous, she couldn't help thinking, *Is it the beihir guarding his prize?*

Brianna put her back against the rock and darted her flashlight around, attempting to see what lurked nearby. *Was it a shark?* She should have looked up if great white sharks ever came to this area. She tapped Nathan frantically, who was still studying the rock carving.

Maybe she should have brought a trident for safety. That would be easier than a harpoon to use in close quarters. Although, a harpoon would be better for a massive underwater beast that wanted to eat them. She should have brought both. That way, she could have carried one in each hand.

Brianna's light caught a flash of a fin attached to a large, dark shape swimming straight toward her.

Chapter 29

Naked Woman

Brianna

Back aboard the boat, Nathan laughed about the curious seal that had befriended Brianna, while Brianna glowered. She knew this rock island was a favorite sunning spot for the local seals, but that one had certainly caught her off guard.

Nathan said, "You know, if we find your seal friend's pelt lying about, we can hide it and it will trap her as a human and she won't be able to return to the sea." Being seeped in the local folklore was rubbing off on them. It was interesting being in a place with such an incredible history and generations of people trying to explain away the mysteries of life, but it would be nice to be home where selkies weren't a part of their daily conversations.

Brianna furrowed her eyebrows at Nathan. She held onto the sides of the boat, relieved to be back inside it. "You're just jealous. I bet that is a one-of-a-kind man selkie who is so handsome that he will sweep me off my feet. I'll keep the selkie's pelt, and you will be sorry that you ever took me out into this forsaken sea."

Nathan wisely held his tongue as he pulled in the anchor and pointed the boat north toward the closest marina. They watched the seals climb up onto the rocky island and sun themselves as the invading boat drove away.

Nathan was the first to speak. "I talked with Dugan this morning and got another update. The hurricane is supposed to hit Riley's Paradise Island tomorrow. Everyone is evacuating the surrounding areas now too."

Brianna frowned. "I'm sorry, Nathan. Are you okay? It can't feel good to know that your home is in imminent danger."

Nathan glanced at her. "It's your home too. We can rebuild the house and the traps. I just wanted you to know that it might take some time. Life might not be how we planned for the foreseeable future. We definitely won't have the staff we started hiring there. We may not have running water or electricity for a while. I don't even know when we will return home."

Brianna hugged herself as a shiver ran through her. She stiffened her chin and pursed her lips. "Things may not always look exactly how we plan them, but I understand that if we work together, we can handle any storm."

After returning the boat, they grabbed a quick lunch at the marina before driving back to their castle. On the drive back, Nathan got a call from work. The vice president apologized for bugging him on his honeymoon, but he really needed him to weigh in on how he wanted the latest emergency at Riley's Games handled. Nathan agreed to call him back as soon as he was back on his computer.

They were within a five-minute walk of home when they spotted Jackson a few yards from the road. He was taking a walk through a field of assorted wildflowers with Jenna on his shoulders. She held an entire bouquet in her hands above her uncle's head. Nathan pulled the car off the road to greet them.

Jenna immediately squealed. "Daddy! Brianna! You're back! Did you find the treasure?"

Nathan pulled the darkened silver key out of his pocket and held it up. "We didn't find the treasure, but we have a key. There must be one last clue on the map that we're missing. We've solved all the riddles and found all the symbols. I'm not sure what we overlooked."

Brianna cocked her head as she asked, "What are you two up to?"

Jackson spoke up. "There have been so many rainy days around here that we decided we must take advantage of this beautiful one. Would you two like to take a walk with us?"

Nathan looked at Brianna and winced. "I'm sorry. I have to jump into some meetings for work this afternoon. You know I've tried to keep my working hours to a minimum while we're here, but there are a few things that I need to handle. You can join them if you want to."

Brianna thought for a moment. She wasn't in the mood to just sit around in the castle twiddling her thumbs on such a nice day. "Sure, I would love to come. Do you guys have a specific destination in mind, or are you just going wherever the road takes you?"

Jackson pointed in the direction they just drove from. "Have you guys checked out the top of the ocean bluffs yet? According to Nathan's new maps, we were going to follow this road and cut through a bit of field and forest to get there. Should be a few miles round-trip walk." He winked at Brianna. "I've heard that the view is amazing."

Brianna rolled her eyes at Jackson. "We were at the base of the bluffs and have driven by the tops, but I admit I am curious to see what the view from the top of the bluffs is really like. It's not too far from the forest. Maybe another half-hour walk. Nathan, would you prefer we waited for you for that adventure?"

Nathan looked at Jackson and ran a hand through his hair but shook his head. "No, you guys have fun. We can plan to have a nice dinner when you guys get back."

Jackson did his best to entertain the two ladies as they walked through the forest. They may not have seen many forest critters, but all the laughing made the walk go quickly. When they finally made it through the trees, they had a last highway to cross before they came to the bluffs.

They stayed a few feet from the sheer drop-off. Brianna caught her breath as she took in the expanse. Water crashed upon the shoreline. She spotted the rocky outcropping they'd boated to earlier that day and a few boats sailing on the deep, dark sea. Water spread out unending to the horizon. It was breathtaking.

Jenna exclaimed over the view. "Look, Brianna! Is that a seal or a dolphin out there?"

"Good eyes, Jenna! Although, I'm not sure, sweetheart. We're so high up that it's kind of hard to tell. It could be either."

Jackson held Jenna tightly on his shoulders. He leaned over to whisper to Brianna. "You know, it's kind of funny, but I think that rock island out there looks like a naked woman."

Brianna smiled to herself. *Everything probably reminds Jackson of a naked woman.* That didn't stop Brianna from taking another look at the rocky outcropping. From above, it did kind of look like a woman lying on her side. There was even a bump out that looked like a breast. It kind of looked like she was pointing. Pointing right toward them.

Chapter 30

Blind Date

Nathan

Nathan scrolled through his phone, checking on the news from back home. There was a video posted earlier in the day from a newscaster. He couldn't get a hold of Dugan, and he needed an update on the hurricane. He pressed play.

A young man stood under an overhang as chaos reigned behind him. Rain poured from the sky as branches whipped around his face. "It looks like the hurricane has made landfall. Winds are starting at eighty-five miles an hour, and unfortunately, we're going to have to evacuate soon like most of the locals. It's only going to get stronger from here. Experts expect winds to get up to one hundred and ten to one hundred and twenty miles an hour. We should expect devastating damage, including damage to houses, uprooted and snapped trees, and road blockages. Stay tuned for more updates as the storm progresses."

Nathan sat, shocked. There had been a few hurricanes that had come by, but none had been this bad in his lifetime. The mainland was being destroyed, and his island was even more susceptible to the hurricane's wrath. What would his island look like? Would there be a home to go back to?

Visions filled his head of coming home from their castle honeymoon. Instead of finding the safe, relaxing paradise they called home, downed trees would have flattened the island. Instead of his safe compound, there would only be rubble. They would have to start over.

Nathan shook his head. It wasn't like him to stress about things he couldn't change.

He would take care of his family, come what may. Right then, he needed to focus on wooing his wife. It was hard shifting from being a single dad to a married man again, and the start of his marriage to Brianna reflected that. Between work and home, he had gotten used to calling all the shots, but he was trying to be more open-minded for her. He loved her too much to do anything less.

"Can I take this off yet?" Brianna asked. She sat in the car next to Nathan, blindfolded.

Nathan smiled to himself. "Trust me. We will be there soon."

"Did you really have to blindfold me this entire car ride? I've had this thing on a good half-hour now and it's getting itchy. What if I just put it on when we get closer?"

Nathan patiently replied, "No. I don't want any of the signs to ruin your surprise. Five more minutes, I promise."

Before the five minutes was up, Nathan parked the car. He got out of his seat and walked around the car to open Brianna's door. "This way, milady."

Brianna grumbled as she got out of the car. She stood still with her hand on her door. "You don't do anything the easy way, do you? Most normal people would have simply said, 'Hey, Brianna, my brother said he would babysit Jenna. Want to head over to Beihir's pub for dinner?' Instead, you decide to pull a cloak-and-dagger stunt where you kidnap me and whisk me off to the unknown. Are our lives ever going to be normal?"

Nathan laughed. "Probably not. If you were looking for normal, you wouldn't have married me."

Nathan led her down a wooded trail, still blindfolded. He guided her feet over roots and gently nudged her shoulders to direct her when the path turned. "Has this turned into some kind of trust walk, or are you taking me to dump my body somewhere? You're lucky I trust you. I get to blindfold you on the way back, right?"

Nathan chuckled. "I guess this is sort of like a trust walk. I was just thinking of your surprise. If you really want to blindfold me on the way back, you can, but it will be dark, so there will be another layer of challenge."

Nathan felt the wind pick up. Brianna's hair was whipping around her head wildly, and he had to move his own head to keep from being slapped in the face. Nathan walked Brianna to the spot with the best view and then took the blindfold off. She looked over the cliff and down onto the rolling hills of green. There were tiny sheep grazing in the fields, and beyond them, the ocean glittered as the sun hit the ocean's ripples.

Brianna gasped. "It's beautiful!" Nathan smiled as he watched her. Tonight was a success. She was pleased. He wanted a lifetime of making her smile.

Nathan pointed at a spot beyond the fields of green. "Do you see that rectangle not too far from the ocean bluff? That's where we've been staying. He smiled at her. "I knew you would enjoy a view of this breathtaking land."

Nathan took off his backpack, pulled out a blanket, and laid it on the ground. He settled down on it, and Brianna sat next to him. He pulled out a bottle of wine and two glasses that were carefully wrapped.

"Thank you for doing this for me," Brianna said, "I'm sorry I've been so quick to argue lately. It's taken me a while to work out how to be married and still be myself. Thank you for being patient with me and taking the time to do special things like this just for me. I know you love me for me, and you won't give up on our marriage, even when things get hard."

Nathan smiled at Brianna. "You were right. I was bossing you around instead of treating you like my wife. Truly, I am trying to make it up to you, but never doubt me. I love you, Brianna, and I always will."

Brianna laid her head on Nathan's shoulder, and he wrapped one of his arms around her as they both looked out over the view. "I love you too, Nathan, and I'm sorry I moved into a different bedroom. We will still fight, but I don't want to run away every time it gets hard. I am in this marriage 'til death do us part."

After listening to his heartbeat for a few moments, she slowly added, "I know you've been sleeping in the room I moved into the last few nights, but would you like to help me move my things back into your room? The one we originally shared when we came here?"

Nathan grinned larger than he had all night. "You bet. I will have you in my bed tonight!" He squeezed her tighter to his side. "You can't change your mind now."

They watched the view in silence for a while as they sipped their wine. Nathan felt like he was finally getting things right. After her glass was empty, Brianna sat up and looked Nathan in the eyes.

"Nathan?" Brianna said.

He poured her another glass, hoping she would snuggle back up against him. "Hmmm?"

"Have there been any updates on the hurricane? Our home?" She looked at him with wide eyes, so trusting. The desire to provide for and protect this woman surged through Nathan, but he knew she was strong. She could handle the truth.

After running his hand through his hair, he said, "The storm hit the mainland just today. The people on shore are losing their roofs and decks as we speak. Dugan won't be able to assess the damage on our island until after everything calms down."

Brianna took a deep breath and spoke in a small, quiet voice. "Okay."

Nathan hesitated before continuing. "The thing is, when hurricanes come through, they're always worse on the island. It has less protection and is just far enough off shore to be right in the middle of the storm sometimes. I don't know how to say this, but we may not have a home to go back to. If anything survives, it will take weeks to months to restore everything to safe living conditions."

Brianna looked at Nathan with tears in her eyes. "I'm so sorry. I know you love your home. You must be heartbroken at the thought of remaking so many of your traps and puzzles. But paradise is anywhere that has you and Jenna. We will survive this and work through whatever we find at the end of the storm."

The two sat in silence for a while as the sun set. Orange and pink streaked across the sky, and a purple hue hung onto the few clouds above them. Nathan couldn't contain himself at the love he felt for his wife. "You are my paradise too," he said softly.

Nathan lowered his head and kissed Brianna with every ounce of his being as the sun set and rays of purple, pink, red, and orange spread across the sky. She kissed him back with such intensity that Nathan was glad they were finally alone. Nathan's kissing soon veered from her lips down her neck. He loved to feel her shiver under his touch, and her soft moans ignited his own passions. Their emotional need for one another drove their physical needs to a whole new level as the last of the light faded.

He drove Brianna home in the moonlight. Both laughed and shared their thoughts on their adventures so far. They talked about the treasure map, both of them more receptive than they had been since arriving in Scotland. Brianna told him about her thoughts on the map when they were flying to Scotland. Nathan talked about his research that led him to find the cave, and later, they talked about her walk with Jackson and Jenna down to the bluffs.

Everything clicked into place. Nathan knew where the treasure was. Could they get there before it was too late?

Chapter 31

Beihir's Treasure

Nathan

Two days later, they were ocean bound again. Nathan wiped the salty water off his brow. He drove their rented motorboat toward the cave entrance, while Brianna watched the sun rise. The water was choppy, but it was still beautiful, and they were finally at the end of their treasure hunt.

He looked over at Brianna; her face was pale, and she was holding onto her seat with a firm grip. Was she seasick or afraid? She was fine when they took out the boat less than a week ago. Maybe it was just too early for her. She wasn't too pleased about waking up before dawn today. She was so stressed over this map business that he felt like, lately, she would just sleep the day away if he let her. After they found the treasure, he would take her somewhere more relaxing. Maybe Brianna would jump back to her normal energetic self.

He felt bad, but he really had no choice but to wake her if they were going to finish this journey together. Going by boat while the tide was still going down was the only way to get to the cave before the tide was back out. Last time, once they walked all the way down there, the tide was already rising. They needed more time to explore before the tide covered the shoreline. Since there were over six hours between low and high tide, they would have plenty of time to search.

Nathan spotted the small, rocky island that looked like a woman pointing to shore. From this angle, it looked just like an ordinary rocky outcropping, but now that Brianna pointed it out, he noticed a section of rock jutting out toward the shoreline. Brianna pointed in the same direction, and Nathan nodded to her. He saw the cave mouth. He turned the boat in toward shore and slowed their arrival.

A few yards off shore, he stopped the boat completely and put down an anchor and a ladder. "We will have to swim to shore from here. There are too many rocks to get any closer safely." *I wish I had thought up some kind of trap to ensure that no one steals it while we're exploring inside the cave.*

Nathan pulled on his wetsuit and turned to Brianna, who was still struggling into hers. He helped her and then slung a small backpack on his back with a few essential supplies that they may need in the cave, including the silver key they found. Luckily, he thought ahead, and it was mostly full of things that could survive when they got wet. The few things that weren't waterproof, he'd sealed in plastic before they left. "Are you ready to jump?"

Brianna looked over the edge, unsure. She was still pale. Jackson had been desperate to come with them, but Nathan had needed someone to stay back at the castle and watch Jenna. Things were going so well between them. He wanted to finish their honeymoon adventure together, but maybe he should have offered that she could stay back while he took Jackson. Was he being bossy again?

Nathan knew how stubborn his wife was. If he as much as suggested she needed any kind of aid, she had to do it all herself. "Are you coming, or do you need some help?" He took a step toward her.

Brianna narrowed her eyes at him. "If you think I'm going to let you feed me to the sharks again..." She jumped into the water, and he watched her swim for shore. She could stand after only going a few feet.

Nathan smiled to himself and plunged into the water below. Apparently, he could not feed her to the sharks, but she would willingly feed them herself if he insinuated that she wasn't capable of doing something by herself. *What an infuriating, lovely woman I married.*

Dripping wet, they arrived on the rocky shore outside of the cave entrance. Nathan opened his backpack to get out their spelunking gear. He placed a hard hat with a light on Brianna's head and put one on himself. After adjusting the lights, the two entered the cave, leaving their wetsuits on to stay warm.

"I think the smell of this bat poop is going to make me sick," Brianna said quietly behind him.

Nathan frowned and turned to give her a half-smile. "Guano may be smelly, but it makes fantastic plant fertilizer. Remember not to make any loud sounds or sudden movements so we don't scare these furry little guys."

Brianna groaned behind him. *I guess the smell really is bothering her.*

Nathan paused and pulled a handkerchief out of his bag. "It's not much, but it might help with the smell a bit.

Brianna grasped it, but he still heard her gagging behind him every once in a while. They combed the front part of the cave but saw no signs of any clues toward finding the treasure.

Nathan felt giddy. *Now it's time to explore the tunnels. We didn't make it this far when we were here last time. A new adventure exploring a mysterious cave and following a treasure map. How could a honeymoon get any better than this? Brianna loves puzzles. She mastered Riley's Paradise Island like she was born there, and she seemed so excited to follow the treasure map on our honeymoon. She's got to be loving this, right?*

They descended deeper and deeper into the depths of the earth. At one point in time, Brianna slipped on the wet stone beneath her feet.

He wasn't fast enough to catch her, but she seemed all right when he helped her up. There was a small tear in her wetsuit, but she hadn't hurt herself.

Eventually, they came to a fork in the cave system. Nathan looked around for any kind of clue about which tunnel they should take. "Do you remember anything from the map that would help us choose a tunnel?"

Brianna pursed her lips. "What if it's hidden somewhere, like the map?" She went around pushing and yanking on every piece of rock that stuck out farther than the rest.

"We can't just go around pushing on every piece of rock in this entire cave system. There has to be some kind of pattern that we missed."

"I think we should go left," Brianna decided.

"What's your reasoning?"

"I think most people would go right." Brianna walked down the left branch of the cave.

Nathan argued, "That's not a good enough reason!" but he quickly followed her. *Just remember, you love her.*

They walked on for a while longer. Brianna tripped over something, but luckily, this time Nathan was ready to catch her. Thankfully, the smell of guano wasn't nearly as strong, and Brianna's normal perky personality abounded.

"Maybe we need to wait for a really severe storm. When the cave fills with water, we could come scuba diving in here to find the treasure," Brianna pondered aloud.

Surprised, Nathan asked, "Would you really want to go scuba diving in here?"

Brianna frowned. "Well, no. I was just trying to think outside the box."

They heard running water as they entered a humongous chamber half filled with water. An underground waterfall fell about fifty feet above them down into the pool. They shone their lights around, trying to take in the breathtaking view. Unfortunately, their headlamps only allowed them to see small parts of the magnificent room at a time.

"If I was going to hide treasure, I would choose this room," Nathan said in awe.

Brianna walked toward the waterfall and let the freezing cold water fall upon her wetsuit. "That's precisely why this is a terrible place to hide treasure. A good place to hide it would be a boring little knob in the wall that people would pass a hundred times without thinking about it twice. Although, I guess it wouldn't hurt to check it out."

Nathan walked over to the waterfall and waded straight into the water. This reminded him of the waterfall outside of Loch Hernessy. Maybe Kiddle had a thing for waterfalls.

Brianna cleared her throat and bit her bottom lip. "Nathan, where are you going?"

Instead of answering, Nathan gave her a smile and then dove the rest of the way under the water. He resurfaced behind the waterfall and heard Brianna calling his name. He didn't mean to worry her.

He yelled through the falls, "Don't worry, I'm fine. I'm just on the other side of the waterfall."

Nathan looked around and noticed a shelf cut into the smooth stone behind the falls. He made his way closer, and sure enough, there was a small, tarnished silver box sitting on the shelf. It looked very similar to the plain silver key they found.

Nathan scooped up the box and made his way back to Brianna. He wished he didn't have to get the box wet and hoped it wouldn't ruin whatever was inside. Although, if a bit of water was going to ruin the contents, it would have happened long ago.

Nathan brought the small box to shore and held it over his head for Brianna to see. "I found it! I found the last of the pirate treasure!"

Brianna's eyes grew large as a smile spread across her face. She gave him a hug and a big kiss on the lips. *I need to find pirate treasure more often!* She huddled close to him, as if waiting for him to open the box and spy their hard-sought-after prize.

Nathan held the small plain box in one hand as he used the silver key he had found in the carved beihir's jaws to open the lock. He opened the lid slowly to make sure that it didn't fall apart from age. The inside of the box seemed to be lined with a wax coating to keep its contents safe from water damage.

The anticipation was palpable. He loved feeling the awe and adventure of their last few hours. He looked up at Brianna's eager face and felt desire coursing through his body. Maybe it was just the adrenaline running through his system, but he wanted his wife right there and then.

Once the box was fully open, he and Brianna puzzled over the contents in the semi-darkness. Neither knew what to say.

Chapter 32

Kidnapped

Nathan

Nathan walked through the front door of the castle carrying the small chest gingerly in his hands. Brianna walked in behind him. Both were grinning from ear to ear. He couldn't wait to show Jenna their "treasure."

Jackson ran out to the main entryway. All of his normal smooth charm was gone. His hair was in disarray, and his wide eyes were moving around the room quickly. He looked frantic. "It's Jenna. She's gone. I can't find her anywhere!"

Nathan felt like his heart stopped in his chest. He stood there, frozen. Brianna was the first to react. "Oh, no! Whoever is after our treasure must have kidnapped her!"

Nathan looked at Brianna with his brows furrowed. He felt sick, but that seemed a bit extreme. "Let's not jump to conclusions. There are so many places to hide and multiple exits. She could be anywhere."

He shot a bunch of questions at Jackson, eager to look for her. "How long has she been gone? She loves to hide. Where have you checked?"

Jackson started at the beginning, telling his story hurriedly instead of adding his normal flourishes. "After you guys left, we played ponies, read books, and had cupcakes for lunch. We had a nice heart-to-heart talk, and I swear I only left her alone in her room for maybe ten minutes while I went to my room down the hall to change. We were going to go outside to walk around the castle next." Jackson looked down at his watch. "She's been gone almost an hour now. I looked through all the bedrooms, even venturing into her trap room. I checked the kitchen, the drawing room, the upstairs servants' quarters, and I was just about to look through the caution-taped areas when I heard you guys get home."

Apologetically, he added, "I'm sorry. I know you told me not to let her out of my sight for even a second with all the weird things going on. It was just for a few minutes. At first, I thought she was hiding somewhere, playing a game."

Nathan jumped right into action. "All right. Jackson, I want you to call Hector. If he doesn't answer, I want you to go to his house and get him. I want the two of you to search the area around the castle. Hopefully, she will just be wandering around the castle grounds, but if Brianna's worst-case scenario is true, we need to catch anyone that might try to leave with her." He looked Jackson dead in the eye. "I want you to call Brianna's cell phone every half-hour to give her an update on your part of the search. We have to find her."

Jackson nodded and took off out the door, whipping his cell phone out as he moved.

Nathan turned to Brianna. He handed her the treasure box. "Please take this back to the drawing room. I want you to call the police. Then look around in the main living areas of the castle. Look for anywhere Jenna might hide. When she was younger, she would hide silently behind the curtains and you'd never know she was there. You're going to man the phones and coordinate the search from here." Nathan ran his hand through his hair. "I can't just sit around here and wait. I'm going to go search the secret passageways." His hands were shaking slightly as he pulled out his phone. "We have to find her."

Brianna nodded and caught his gaze. "We will find her."

Nathan tried to hold that reassurance close to his heart as Brianna ran off to the drawing room. *We have to find my little girl. I can't lose her.*

Nathan jogged down the hallway toward the secret passageway. His breathing got faster and shallower. His chest hurt, and he felt dizzy. He stopped before the caution tape.

Am I having a panic attack? He needed to get a hold of himself. His Little Bird needed him, and he had no time to lose. Nathan bent over and tried to take a deep breath. *She's going to be okay. She's probably just playing hide-and-seek or getting into mischief. I'm sure I will find her wandering around in these tunnels.*

Once the worst of the panic subsided, Nathan crossed the caution tape and quickly made his way down the hallway. *I wish we hadn't come through here so much. It would be really helpful if we could see her footprints in the dust still.*

Every once in a while, he caught sight of a small footprint, but they could have been from earlier. He had taken Jenna on an adventure down here to set up the traps at the secret entrance. He sadly smiled to himself, remembering how excited she was.

Nathan called down the hallway, quickly glancing into bedrooms and looking under dilapidated furniture. Another fear seized his heart. *What if she fell into a hole or got hurt somewhere and can't call for help?*

Brownie and a few of the kittens were frolicking around in the hallway but hid as soon as he drew near. He knew little about kittens but guessed they were about four weeks old now. *If Jenna was anywhere, she would be here with them.*

Nathan called once again. "Jenna! Jenna! Are you in here? Just come out, Little Bird, and I won't be mad. I'm so worried." A quick search revealed she wasn't there.

Nathan whipped out the flashlight he'd used in the caves only a few hours ago. He hastened past the tapestry and made his way down the secret passageway.

Eventually, he came to the entrance that led to the forest. He checked on his trap. The alarm and splatter trap were still in place. No one had triggered them. He moved the piece of metal out of the way and stepped outside. There was no sign of anyone.

Nathan quickly called Brianna to update her. Jackson and Hector were searching the grounds but had found nothing yet. It was time to explore the labyrinth of tunnels inside the castle. He didn't know how he was going to keep himself from getting lost.

Nathan went down a few unexplored hallways, desperately trying to keep track of where he was going. There were adult-sized footprints leading in a few different directions that he tried to follow, but he caught no sight of child-sized footprints going through these smaller corridors. *Was someone carrying her?*

He peeked through peepholes, looking into a room that he didn't recall ever seeing. They had only discovered the tip of the secrets of this castle. He felt like the more mysteries they uncovered, the more they were left with.

Just then, Nathan heard a loud *BANG* reverberate throughout the castle. The trap from the secret passageway had been activated. Someone was entering or leaving the tunnels. *I need to get back there immediately!*

Nathan tried to retrace his steps back the way he came, but he recognized nothing. He was helplessly lost.

Chapter 33

Yummy Treasure

Brianna

Brianna shook as she ran from room to room, yelling Jenna's name and double-checking for any signs of the little girl. The police weren't very helpful. They didn't view the case as a huge priority since the little girl had only been missing for an hour.

When she insisted that a kidnapper had probably snuck into the castle and taken her, the policeman tried to reassure her. "Don't jump to any conclusions. Kids do this all the time. We will send someone out, but your daughter will probably make her own way home before we get there."

After a half-hour, Brianna had checked all the rooms of the main castle a second time. No sign of Jenna. Both Nathan and Jackson had called her to check in and neither of them had found Jenna.

She needed to do something. She was feeling nauseous from the stress of just sitting around waiting for Jenna to show up. If Nathan were here right now, what would he do? Inspiration struck, and Brianna excitedly got to work.

Brianna took the treasure chest to the drawing room and placed it on the table. There was only one person she could think of that really gave her a bad feeling. *Florine.*

If Florine wanted treasure, she wouldn't believe that they had found nothing with a large monetary value. Brianna needed to set up her own trap to catch her in the act. *If Florine is the culprit, I need something shiny to catch her attention.*

Brianna opened the small treasure chest. She gently extracted the old journal from Captain Kiddle, a ring that looked like a family seal, and a miniature painting of a young woman. *I'll take these items and secure them in the safe in the pantry.*

She refilled the chest and set up a simple rubber-coated snap trap attached to the table where the chest sat. Nathan couldn't help but pack a few that were smaller than a bear trap and less intense. He'd made them himself, and he'd perfectly sized them for a human. She placed a light rug over the trap and tried to camouflage the bump by moving a pair of Nathan's shoes beside it. She artistically arranged another rug in front of the bump to look like it got slightly bunched up when Nathan kicked off his shoes.

It wouldn't pass a close inspection, but she didn't pin Florine as particularly smart. It didn't have Nathan's normal finesse, but that was the best she could come up with in a few minutes. She hoped Florine would be in a hurry to steal whatever she could find and flounce right into the trap. Hopefully, they would find Florine and save Jenna. Nothing else mattered anyway.

Brianna heard a loud bang. *Uh-oh. Looks like Nathan set off his own trap down there.* Unless... *could it be Florine coming for the treasure?* She had to hurry.

Brianna left the drawing room to secure Captain Kiddle's keepsakes. She made a small, frustrated noise as she started up the stairs. Right then, she wished she didn't have to take the extra step to go upstairs and fish out that key. It was a lot of steps when the safe was downstairs in the kitchen's pantry.

After securing the treasures, Brianna made her way back to the drawing room. Jenna had been gone for two hours now. Brianna should probably check in with everyone and see what happened with the trap that went off. Then she should call and see what was taking the authorities so long.

Brianna opened the door and stood there in shock. Lewis stood in front of the treasure chest. He was covered in red dye and holding the sword that was stolen from the castle wall. He picked up one of the chocolate coins from the treasure chest and threw it on the ground at Brianna's feet.

The kind face she'd come to know vanished as his lips curled into a snarl. "Where is the real treasure? I didn't steal your notebooks and maps and follow you into caves to be tricked by chocolate."

Brianna narrowed her eyes at him. "What have you done with Jenna? Where is she?"

Confusion crossed Lewis's face, and his eye twitched. "Don't try your trickery on me. We both know I don't have Jenna. Just give me the real treasure and I will leave without hurting you."

Brianna grimaced. "Actually, you already stole the only real treasure we found. Those three silver coins you took were the only things of value in the whole lot."

Anger flashed as Lewis scrunched up his face so much that his brows almost met in the middle. He waved the sword. "What are you trying to do here? You can't flip the tables on me. I'm the one with the weapon. We both know that I did nothing to your little girl, and I didn't steal any coins. Now give me the treasure!" Lewis moved toward Brianna threateningly.

Brianna raised her hands. "Leave me alone. I'm going to move toward the table to get you what you want."

Lewis watched her carefully but must have been more interested in where she was going than keeping the sword pointed straight at her. The sword sagged.

Brianna spoke calmly as she inched toward the table. "I know you say that you didn't kidnap Jenna and you didn't take the coins, but I just have one more question. How did you steal the maps when we saw you working at the festival?"

Lewis took a step backwards toward the table containing the treasure chest, keeping her in sight. His lips curled as he spoke. "That wasn't me at the Folklore Fair. I enjoy a good historical sword when I see it, but I don't waste my time with things like folklore or doing demonstrations for free. The person you saw was my brother, Callum. He's a year older than me, but people mistake us for twins all the time. That sucker would have probably given you his coat just to be kind. For me, it was the perfect excuse to gain your trust and a reasonable excuse to stop by and 'help' with your treasure map."

He narrowed his eyes as Brianna took another step forward. Lewis said, "I don't think it's fair that a pair of outsiders would come here and steal a piece of our history. I've lived here all my life. If someone finds this treasure, it should be me."

Lewis took another step back. *Snap!* The hidden trap caught his foot, and the surprise tripped him. Lewis's mouth dropped open as he let out an eardrum-shattering screech.

The sword went skittering across the carpet, and both Lewis and Brianna lunged for it. Lewis would have beaten her there, but he was stopped when his foot tugged on its tether attached to the table.

The table shifted under the force of his leap. The treasure chest fell from the table onto the ground, spilling chocolate coins all around Lewis.

Brianna pointed the sword at him. "Snack on all the chocolate you want as you wait for the police. If you try to make a wrong move, I will stab you! In fact, my nerves are so far gone right now that I might just stab your leg if you look at me funny."

Quickly, she called the police on her cell phone while trying to hold the sword steadily. Before she could finish dialing them, they burst through the door.

Chapter 34

House of Destructions

Brianna

T he stress of the last two hours had made Brianna so exhausted that she prayed with all her might that they would find Jenna. She would never let that little girl out of her sight again. She would never stop fighting for her. They simply had to find her. Lewis continued to tell the police that he hadn't even seen the little girl since he arrived that day.

Brianna called Nathan. "Hey, Nathan..."

Frantically, Nathan interrupted her. "What was that screaming? Are you and Jenna okay?"

Brianna paused. She didn't want to tell him that his baby girl was still missing. "I'm okay. It was Lewis. He snuck in through the back passageway, trying to steal the treasure. The police are here now. They have him in custody... but he claims he doesn't have Jenna."

A call waiting beeped on her phone. Jackson was trying to get a hold of her. "Listen, Nathan. I have to go. Jackson is calling. Don't give up hope."

Nathan, normally a sea of calm, sounded more panicked than she had ever heard him before. His breathing picked up pace as if he was jogging. "I searched as much as I could down here in the secret tunnels. I finally found my way back to the main path. Talk to Jackson. I'll be there in a few minutes."

Brianna hung up with Nathan. She'd missed Jackson's call and had to call him back. He didn't answer. She tried him again. He didn't answer. How dare that man choose not to answer his phone right now?

She went outside the castle courtyard to see if she could spot him. Brianna found him and beheld the most beautiful sight she had ever seen. She would give up every mountain vista, seashore paradise, and waterfall reverie for the rest of her life just for the relief of that moment.

Jackson was a few yards from the castle, carrying Jenna on his shoulders. She looked dirty and had a tiny backpack bouncing on her back, but otherwise seemed fine. She was talking intently into Jackson's ear. He nodded and responded, apparently not realizing Brianna was trying to get a hold of him.

Nathan walked up behind her. She heard a loud sigh of relief. "Oh, thank goodness!"

Jackson spotted them and set Jenna down. Jenna immediately ran up to them, Brianna and Nathan meeting her halfway. They threw their arms around Jenna and held her tightly in a small huddle.

Jenna cried as she clung to her parents. "I don't want to grow up and live in the woods by myself. I'm so sorry I ran away! Please can I come back?"

Brianna's heart broke at the little girl's confusing words. "Jenna, sweetheart. Why did you run away? Why would you think you need to live in the woods? You always have a home with us." She looked Jenna straight in the eyes. "We love you with all of our hearts."

A soft *meow* interrupted their conversation. A tiny white head popped out of the neck hole of Jenna's shirt. Brianna looked closer at Jenna to realize that she had one arm supporting the bottom of the kitten under her shirt.

Nathan gave her another squeeze. "Little Bird, I'm so glad that you're safe. You don't know how worried I was about you and how much I love you. Why don't you start at the beginning? Tell us what's going on."

Jenna cuddled the kitten close to her chest. "Uncle Jack and I were talking. I told him I'm not little anymore, and I don't need a babysitter. I don't want to be called a little bird anymore either. I'm big." Her sniffling got louder as she explained her reasoning. "Uncle Jack told me that someday you might have another baby and I will need to be a big girl to help. He said when I'm even bigger, I would want to have my own house and my own space. Until then, you guys are doing the best you can to love me, watch over me, and teach me." She looked at Nathan with a tear in her eye. "I got mad that you would have another baby to replace me. I decided I was ready to be grown up now so I could make my own rules so I wouldn't have to worry about a baby taking my place. I wanted a kitten, and I wanted to go into the secret tunnels you showed me all by myself, so I did." Jenna shrugged her shoulder, jostling the backpack she was carrying. "I packed my backpack with all of my underwear and a flashlight. Then I went to the kitchen to get a container of chicken for me and my new kitten to eat."

Jenna held the kitten up to her face, still keeping the rest of it cuddled under her shirt. The kitten squirmed and disappeared back under Jenna's shirt. It actually looked like Jenna had an undershirt on and a t-shirt over the top to create a little pouch for the kitten. They watched the kitten move around under the shirt until it finally settled down again.

The little girl wouldn't look either Nathan or Brianna in the eye as she described the next part. "I went up to the caution tape and went over it all by myself, even though I knew you wouldn't want me to.

Then I went to get one of Brownie's kittens, but they all hid. I finally trapped this one behind a curtain."

Jenna finally stopped sniffling as she talked about the kitten. "She scratched me at first, but I made a bed for her under my shirt with some of my underwear and fed her some chicken. She is much calmer now. I named her Cupcake. She was going to be my new pet in the house I was going to build beside the stream.

"I went through the secret passageway, but it was a lot scarier without you with me, Daddy." Jenna gave Nathan another snuggle. "When I got to the end, I remember how you showed me the trap you set. I stepped around the pressure points, just like you showed me to do back at home on our island." Jenna looked at Nathan through her eyelashes. "I was getting scared and thought that maybe I wasn't ready to live on my own. I knew if I went back, you would be mad at me for disobeying and make me return Cupcake, so I kept going." With arms wrapped around her middle, Jenna sniffed. "Cupcake and I sat by the stream for a while. I cried because I didn't know how to make my own house, and we ran out of chicken. We were getting hungry, but I couldn't go home. I decided we were just going to live in the woods and eat worms. Then I heard Uncle Jack call my name. I knew he would make me feel better."

Nathan hugged her tight. "Jenna, I'm sorry you felt replaced. It's just been you and me for a long time now, so I can see why you would get scared. Don't worry. We aren't planning on having a baby anytime soon. Someday, if we decide to, that little one would never take your place. It would just grow our family larger. You should have told me you don't want to be called Little Bird anymore. I know you're growing up, but it's hard on me too. Just talk to me, Jenna."

Brianna was looking over every part of the little girl to make sure she was all right. Other than a few scratches, she seemed to be fine after her adventures. She petted the kitten that lay against Jenna's stomach. "Sweetheart, this kitten is too little to be away from his mommy. We can look into getting you a pet when we get settled back at home, but we can't take on the responsibility of another animal right now when it might be a while before we can go home again."

Jenna hung her head and sniffled. "But I love her."

After giving Jenna a small half-smile, Brianna gave her another hug, making sure not to squeeze the kitten. "I know you do, but her mommy loves her too, and right now, this kitten still needs her mommy's milk to feed her. She's not ready to live on her own and eat chicken. Would you like to help me find a home for her with the people from town?"

"She needs to be looked after by a little girl," Jenna said.

Shaking her head, Brianna smiled. "We'll try. You know, no matter what happens with me and your daddy, you will always be your daddy's special girl. Please don't run away again. It terrified us because we love you so much."

They stood together in silence for a while, happy to have their little family in one place. Brianna said, "I think any place where we are all together is paradise."

Nathan bopped Jenna's nose. "Now that I can't call you Little Bird anymore, does that mean I can call you Big Bird?"

Jenna rolled her eyes. "Dad!"

Brianna laughed and held her family tight.

Chapter 35

Captain Kiddle's Secrets

Brianna

Brianna shut the door behind the police that were leaving and jiggled two silver coins in her hand. She walked to the drawing room where Nathan was sitting at the large table. He was studiously poring over Captain Angus Kiddle's journal.

Brianna dropped the coins on the book directly in front of him. "Look what the police dropped off."

Nathan lifted his head. He picked the coins up and held them up to the light to examine them more closely. "Where did they find our treasure? Only two?"

Jenna, who was previously playing with her ponies on the floor, perked up and ran over to the table. "Our pirate treasure! You got it back! Hooray!"

Nathan smiled at her as he let her examine the coins. "Yes, Little... I mean, Jenna. It looks like we got some of the treasure back, but we would trade it all in a second to make sure that you are safe and sound with us."

Brianna slouched in the enormous stuffed chair. *I need a vacation from this honeymoon. I think I'm burned out from all the treasure hunting and suspense. Lately, I just feel so tired all the time.*

Brianna answered from her reclined position, "The police said they picked them up at a local pawn shop and verified that the seller was Lewis. He must have snuck into the castle a few times while we were staying here. They are going to keep an eye out for the last coin and your map notes while they finish up their burglary investigation.

Bored with their talk, Jenna went back to play with her ponies. They were currently galloping across the rug, racing from one side to the other, searching for a lost baby pony. *Kids really do process everything through play.*

Nathan pointed to the journal. "You should read Kiddle's journal. It's pretty fascinating. Some of these entries talk about his childhood and having to grow up and serve the same people who stole his home. The first section is pretty rough and full of a lot of anger." He focused is eyes back down at the journal and looked for a specific spot a few pages back. "What's really interesting is seeing his transformation of character. After he was a privateer for a while and built up a reputation, he came back to Dugan Castle. The servants secreted him back in, but instead of slaughtering the current masters of the castle, he forgave them and let them leave. He realized the servants were his family in that they had raised and cared for him."

He read from the journal. "'My sweet primrose. I yearn for you and await the moment we can be together. My reputation may make some men tremble, but my lips yearn only to make you shiver from anticipation. I will make my fortunes so that your father sees me as worthy when I ask for your hand.'"

Nathan looked up and explained, "These aren't the words of an angry, murderous privateer. He fell in love and was planning on taking one last trip to a faraway place with warm climates to make his riches. His plan was to come back and marry the woman he loved and provide for her in the manner she was accustomed to."

Nathan pointed to the copy of the map that lay under his book. "I think Kiddle got stranded for whatever reason on our island and never made it back. I think he settled on the island and made this map so his progeny could someday find the treasures he left behind in his privateering days."

Brianna contemplated the story Nathan told her. It was so long ago that there was a lot of guesswork on their part. What they knew made a pretty fascinating story. "After such a tragic life, I hope he found his paradise in the end."

Nathan nodded. "Yeah, I hope so too. There is a weird pattern to some words in here. Maybe I will find out more from studying it at home." Nathan's phone buzzed. "Speaking of home, it looks like Dugan sent us some pictures. Curious that he didn't call."

There was silence as Nathan swiped through a dozen pictures. Not wanting to be left out, Brianna got up and walked over to the table. Nathan's brows furrowed as he solemnly pushed the phone toward her and crossed his arms.

The first picture showed the dock on Riley's Paradise Island utterly destroyed, with pieces of wood lying around on the beach and floating in the water. The next few pictures were of their home, that they lovingly called the compound.

A tree was lying on top of the house. Roof tiles, downed trees, branches, and even a piece of furniture were lying around the compound haphazardly. *Is that an end table lying out there?* Pictures of the inside showed a tree had fallen into one of the upstairs bedrooms that she used to make her glass animals. The room was a disaster area of water damage and debris. The kitchen showed a branch that had crashed through the window. It was a mess, but at least it looked salvageable.

The next picture was of the secret garden. Brianna knew they had previously evacuated all the animals, but their home was a different matter. There were branches and leaves lying inside the garden, but the high garden wall seemed to have protected it from the worst of the storm. Even the greenhouse seemed to have withstood minimal damage. Maybe they could camp out there if they really needed to. She pictured being woken up by a goat trying to eat her hair.

The last few images were of Jackson's and their father's home. Hurricane Karen hit it the hardest. The whole top floor was missing and only a few walls remained on the main floor. Pieces of broken furniture littered the entire area. Nathan's childhood home was demolished.

Brianna stared at the phone. Her eyes glazed over, and she no longer truly saw the pictures. She felt like she needed to throw up. *We are homeless.*

Nathan grimaced, watching her reaction. "We only have a month left at this castle, but I think we need to extend our vacation. I would like to make plans to go out to California and visit my Aunt Priscilla for a while. What do you think?"

Brianna nodded and collapsed in a heap back in her chair.

Chapter 36

The Game of Love

Brianna

Brianna smiled as her best friend, Mavis, sat on the floor with Jenna. Her spiky red hair bounced about her head as she galloped a play pony to Jenna. Too tired to do more than sit in a chair and watch, Brianna felt like she needed to sleep for a week straight to get back to her normal self.

After a while, Mavis got up and slouched in the chair next to Brianna. "You poor thing. You look horrible. I'm sorry I missed all the excitement last week. You have been through a lot."

A small smile spread across her lips. "Things have definitely been crazy since we got to Scotland, but now that I have you here, everything seems calmer."

Mavis threw back her head and laughed. "Honey, I'm pretty pooped from jet lag right now, but have you ever known me to be calm? I only get to spend a week in this beautiful place before I have to return to that viper's nest of a job. I intend to take full advantage of this trip and enjoy every second! You need to show me those secret tunnels, and then I found a place nearby where we can go gorge scrambling, and if we want, we can go cliff jumping after that..."

Brianna held up her hand. "Mavis, hold on a second. We will take you to see all the sights, but for now, do you want to get settled in a room and have some lunch? I'm surprised the first place on your list wasn't the local pub. I thought you would look for a handsome Scotsman now that you broke up with your boyfriend."

A grimace crossed Mavis's face. "I've sworn off men! They act all nice and sweet and then they make your life miserable. I have decided that I would much prefer to be a spinster than deal with the likes of men anymore."

Her friend had never gone more than a few weeks without a new guy. It would be interesting to see how long this "spinsterhood" lasted. Brianna laid her hand on Mavis's shoulder. "You poor thing. He must have really broken your heart."

Quietly, Mavis said, "Yeah. I thought he was the one."

Apparently, Mavis was done with talking about herself, because she hopped out of her chair and hauled Brianna up. "Come on! Stop being such a bump on a log. I need a tour of this place. I'm in a castle and all you have shown me is one little room." She called over to Jenna, "Do you want to give me a tour, Jenna?"

Jenna jumped up. "Yippee! I can't wait to show you my bedroom and my trap room and the kittens..."

Brianna chuckled. "It looks like you guys have outmaneuvered me. Food and naps will have to wait. A tour it is!"

Before they made it to the door, Jackson strode into the room. He stopped still when he spotted Mavis. "Mavis! It's so nice to see you. A night hasn't passed without dreaming of the beauty who lit up our island with her fiery-red hair at Nathan's wedding. Well, I guess Brianna also had fiery hair that night..."

Mavis held up her hand with her palm facing Jackson, stopping him short. "Nope. Not going there. Save your breath." Then she walked past him without another glance. Brianna laughed to see Jackson's slackened features as he stared after Mavis, speechless, before she followed her.

Jenna ran up to Jackson and hugged his legs. "We're taking Mavis on a tour of the castle! Want to come?"

Jackson shook his head, but his eyes never left the disappearing figure of Mavis. "No, not right now. I'll catch up with you guys later. You have fun."

Jenna ran to catch up with the two women. "Can we go to my trap room first? Please?"

Brianna smiled. "Sure. Lead the way." They followed Jenna, who hopped up the stairs two at a time.

Turning to Mavis, Brianna asked, "Still no luck with your job search?"

Mavis shook her head. "No. I have had a few interviews, but nothing has been a good fit. People are having babies every day. I thought it would be easy to get a job as a midwife when I got certified, but most places either want to hire a nurse or a doctor. I could be a doula, but I want to do more than that. Now that you're gone and things are done with my boyfriend, there really isn't much holding me in that area. I'm thinking of moving." She gave Brianna a smile. "Maybe I'll even find a job at a beach closer to a certain best friend I hardly get to see anymore."

On the top floor, on their way to Jenna's trap room, they passed Nathan. He nodded his head at Mavis. "I'm glad to see you made it safely. Brianna has been counting the minutes until you arrived."

Mavis gave Brianna a side hug. "Yes, I miss this girlie. You better keep taking good care of her or I might steal her back."

Nodding, Nathan said, "I will make sure of it."

Nathan's phone rang, and he held up a finger. "If you girls would excuse me, this is Dugan. I really need to talk to him."

Brianna waved him to go. "Sure, just let me know what he says."

After answering the phone, she overheard the beginning of their conversation. "Are you sure it's safe to head back to the island?... Did you just say that you're already there and the employee you couldn't get a hold of is there as well? We aren't ready for her. Did you send her home?" That sure sounded intriguing. Brianna would have to find out what that conversation was all about later.

They stopped behind Jenna at her trap room, and the little girl carefully opened the door. Mavis gasped. "My, you have been busy in there. I don't think I could even get into that room. Please tell me you plan to have me sleep in a different bed."

Jenna let out a squeal. "Hooray! I finally caught one!" As lithe as could be, she climbed over chairs and squirmed under ropes until she stopped at a small end table that sat in the middle of the room. On it sat an overturned basket that had originally been held up by a stick.

Jenna jumped up and down. "I did it! I did it! I finally caught a brownie to clean my room." Carefully, Jenna lifted the basket only a quarter of an inch and moved her face close to peer inside.

She laughed as she lifted the basket the rest of the way off. There sat a small plate with a large chocolate brownie in the middle of it, surrounded by gold chocolate coins. Jenna wasted no time taking a bite of the brownie. "It won't clean my room, but it's sure delicious!"

Brianna smiled from the doorway. "Now our trip has officially been a success. Jenna, you caught a brownie, and we have the greatest treasure of all. Our family."

She winked at Mavis. "I have more brownies down in the kitchen if you want some. I may have needed to taste test some, and they are perfectly soft and a little gooey in the middle."

Chapter 37

Surprise!

Nathan

Nathan walked up to his bedroom at Brianna's request. She said there was a gigantic spider on the bed and asked if he would take care of it for her. He walked down the hallway, enjoying the solitude. While it was nice to have Jackson and Mavis here for a while, he was happy to have the place back to himself. Just him and his family.

Nathan walked into his room and picked up a shoe before going over to his bed. Instead of a spider, there was a decorative box sitting on the middle of the quilt. He opened the box to find three chocolate kisses. He smiled. Brianna was really loving her chocolate lately.

He popped one of the chocolate kisses in his mouth and let it slowly melt on his tongue as he pondered. Nathan had proposed to Brianna with a scavenger hunt in a similar box. Maybe Brianna wanted to renew their vows now that they had figured their relationship out.

With that thought in mind, Nathan unwrapped the other two chocolate kisses and examined the wrappers. No clues there. He'd used a trick box with his proposal, so he checked the box for any loose edges.

Aha! The inside bottom of the box wiggled. Upon closer inspection, Nathan realized the box looked significantly shallower than it should be from the outside. Nathan pushed down on one side of the inside of the wooden box and the other end pivoted upwards. Inside was another chocolate kiss.

What was his crazy woman getting at? Should he woo her with more chocolate? Nathan opened the candy and popped that one into his mouth. He looked at the wrapper and saw a tiny delicate map drawn on it.

Nathan rolled his eyes. *This is what I get for trying to do a creative proposal.* Now he had to run around like a wild goose trying to follow clues. It was much more amusing the other way around.

The map had a rectangle that seemed to be the castle and a few trees in one corner. A squiggly line ran through the map. *I bet that is where we had our first picnic along the stream.*

Nathan dragged his feet, getting ready for his excursion. He didn't want to waste such a beautiful day running around by himself. He knew Brianna was busy making more of her series of glass mythical creatures to sell at her next craft fair.

Nathan went and knocked on Jenna's door. "Jenna!" he yelled. "Come on out. We are going on a scavenger hunt."

Nathan heard the pitter-patter of little feet racing to the doorway. Breathlessly, Jenna answered. "Really? That would be so much fun! Let's go!"

Patiently, Nathan eyed her feet. "Why don't you grab some socks and shoes first? I don't think we will get very far otherwise. Our first stop is to our favorite picnic spot near the stream."

Jenna squealed in excitement and took off to find her footwear. After spending much too long looking for a lost left shoe, they were finally ready to go. The two cheerily made their way out of the castle and across the field toward the forest.

Jenna looked at Nathan. "Daddy, did you make the scavenger hunt?"

Nathan shook his head. "No, honey. This is a scavenger hunt Brianna made for us. Any ideas where it will send us next?"

Jenna shouted out ideas. "Maybe we will go to the beihir's cave or the library. Can we go visit the kittens? Please can I have one? They are so cute! I will take care of it and love it so much."

Nathan chuckled at Jenna's change in conversation. "I'm sorry. We can't get a pet right now with our home a mess. We can talk about it again when things settle back down."

Jenna pouted the rest of the way to the stream. She perked up when she heard the water and seemed to forget any wrong committed against her. Nathan searched around the clearing. Sure enough, they were in the right place. Nailed to a tree was an old-fashioned picture of an old man.

Hmmm.... He thought he recognized this picture. He turned the page over and examined the copy of the painting up close. He could find nothing out of the ordinary about the picture. Was the painting on one of the walls of the castle?

Nathan and Brianna walked back to the castle. Nathan wracked his brain, trying to remember where he had seen it. They came up to the courtyard to see Hector cleaning up some rubble.

Nathan called out, "Good morning, Hector! A fine day, isn't it?"

Hector gently smiled at Jenna and nodded his head at Nathan. "Good day, my laird. Out enjoying the sunshine? You only have another week here, am I right?"

Nathan sadly nodded his head. "We have had a lovely visit, but after a brief detour to visit my aunt, we need to return home. To salvage what's left of it."

Hector noticed the picture in Nathan's hands. "What do you have here?"

Jenna piped up, "We found a picture of an old man. Brianna made a scavenger hunt for us. Isn't that exciting!"

Hector shook his head. "You folk and your treasure hunts. A simple life is what I prefer. Can I see it?"

Nathan handed Hector the picture. "Why, I believe that you have a picture of Captain Kiddle here. He used to own that castle." Realization dawned on Nathan. He remembered where he had seen the picture before.

Nathan thanked Hector and rushed off to the hidden passageway that led to the servants' rooms that Brianna had shown him. He smiled. He had to admit that he was getting into this search, and Jenna was hot on his heels.

They made it up to the servants' hallway, and there was the matching picture hanging on the wall. Beside the picture was a small photo of Jenna.

Jenna jumped up and down. "Look, it's me! I'm the prize!"

Nathan smiled. He leaned down and gave Jenna a kiss on the top of her head. "You are definitely the most precious prize."

Nathan flipped the photo over. On the back, Brianna had written "trap maker in training." Jenna definitely was getting better at the traps she was making. In fact, that one bedroom that Brianna let her make into a trap room was impossible to navigate at this point. He might even have to pay to have some of that room remodeled after they left.

"I think the next clue is in your special trap room. Lead the way!"

Jenna rushed out of the servants' area and to the hallway where their bedrooms were located. Nathan did his best to keep up. She flung open her door and carefully crawled on the floor to get under the yarn that covered most of the doorway. Jenna climbed up on top of a stool that blocked her pathway and turned toward her father at the door. "Daddy, aren't you coming?"

Nathan gaped at the room. It shocked him to see thousands of gum bands looped together and hung from the ceiling at different angles. Jenna had strung yarn from wall to wall, zigzagging back and forth throughout the room. She had furniture turned over and moved to fill in any empty spaces between the yarn and gum bands. Obstacles were scattered around on the ground. He saw one section with a collection of marbles and another with jacks that created caltrops. How in the world did Brianna get a clue in there? How would they find anything in all of that?

It had been a while since Jenna had shown off her creations to him in this room. Now it was ten times worse. He didn't know how they were going to clean it up in a week when they went to leave. This room was definitely going to need a new paint job.

Nathan got down on his hands and knees, but the yarn was too close together to fit his adult frame. He could force his way into the room and knock over all of Jenna's hard work. Unfortunately, he felt he would get just as stuck in this spiderweb as Jenna intended.

Nathan peered through the yarn at Jenna's eager face waiting for him. "Jenna, I think Brianna made this part of the scavenger hunt for you. You can do this. I want you to look around for a clue. Anything that looks out of place in your room. Anything that you didn't do or didn't put in here. Can you do that?"

Jenna solemnly nodded. "I won't let you down, Dad. I can do this." She hopped off the stool into a pile of blankets and army-crawled around the room. "All of my yarn looks the same. Do you think she took one of my marbles?"

Nathan thought for a moment. "Jenna, where do you like to play the most when you're in here? Do you have a favorite hiding place or secret tunnel or something?"

Jenna's eyes lit up. "I can check in my secret hideout. I like to take books and read them in there." Jenna climbed up onto a long dresser and crawled across it. She took a leap off the dresser onto the bed, where she squealed with laughter. Then she crawled to the backside of the bed and slid off the bed headfirst onto a pillow. She gently guided her body under the bed and disappeared.

Nathan ran his hand through his hair. That didn't look too safe. He thought he saw a light shine under the bed, but he couldn't see anything under the bed skirt with so many miscellaneous things blocking his way.

Finally, Jenna emerged from under the bed triumphantly. She held up a card. "I found the clue, Dad! I did it! All by myself!" Jenna hopped, climbed, and crawled her way back to the doorway. She handed her dad the card.

The front of the card had a picture of an island paradise that reminded him of home. He opened it. Inside, the left-hand side said, "Good job, Jenna. I knew you could do it!" The right-hand side had a short riddle:

"Struggles and woes, highs and lows. Old becomes new, paradise is with you.

Love gives and takes. Now, let's take time to bake!"

Nathan smiled at Brianna's last word choice. She never was very good at being subtle. Nathan turned to Jenna and read her the poem. "What do you think, Little Bird... erm, I mean, Jenna. Do you think Brianna is sending us to make her some chocolate chip cookies?"

Jenna's eyes twinkled, as if she could not think of a better option in the world. "Yes! Can mine have rainbow sprinkles too?"

Nathan caught a whiff of homemade bread as he neared the kitchen. Yummy. Maybe she made him fresh bread! It smelled so good that his mouth watered. He could almost taste it.

He had built up a bit of an appetite running around doing her scavenger hunt. At least she made lunch. Nathan and Jenna entered the kitchen to find Brianna sitting there calmly drinking a cup of tea.

Nathan smiled at her. "This smells delicious! Jenna got the last clue under the bed in her trap room. How in the world did you get it in there?" Before allowing her to answer, Nathan took another appreciative whiff of the air. "Did you make homemade bread?" Nathan knelt down to get a look through the glass of the oven.

Brianna calmly said, "It's a bun."

Nathan looked at her, confused. "Did you make buns for sandwiches? I know you love a good turkey sandwich."

Brianna sat silently, giving him a few minutes to think. A range of emotions crossed Nathan's face as his eyebrows twisted in confusion, then his eyebrows rose, and his eyes opened wide as excitement lit up his face. Nathan looked over at Brianna for confirmation. She nodded her head and a broad smile crested both of their lips.

Eyes never leaving Brianna, Nathan spoke excitedly to Jenna. "Jenna. We finished the scavenger hunt and received the best prize. It looks like you are going to be a big sister!"

A Note from the Author

Did you enjoy this story?

I would really appreciate your help by leaving a short, honest review in your favorite store. This not only helps me to gain visibility of my stories, but helps other readers find a good book that they would enjoy. Thank you in advance and happy reading!

Hiding Paradise

Book 3 in the Puzzling through Romance Series

Chapter One
Woman Overboard

Gina

Gina looked around wide-eyed at the destruction all around her. *This is the paradise I chose as my refuge? What was I thinking?*

She took a deep breath, squared her shoulders, and turned around to the driver of the boat that gave her a ride. "Thank you so much for bringing me out here. The dock looks like the storm hit it pretty badly, but it's getting shallow. If you can just get me as close to shore as is safe, I will climb down the ladder on the side of your boat and walk to shore through the shallows."

The kindly older man, Chester, who was the captain of the small ocean vessel she rented, furrowed his bushy eyebrows. "Miss, I'm having second thoughts. I agreed to drive you out here, but I can't, in good conscience, leave you here. Hurricane Karen wrecked this island, and if you get off this boat, you will strand yourself. Listen, I know you really wanted to take a trip out here, but that island isn't safe. I'm going to take this boat back to the mainland and I'll give you a refund. I'm retired and don't truly need the income. Besides, a few hundred dollars isn't worth your life."

Gina panicked. "I can't go back. I have to get on this island. Today is my first day of work as the island's chef."

Chester gently shook his graying head. "I'm sorry, Miss. There isn't anyone here. Whoever you were supposed to work for probably evacuated for the hurricane like everyone else."

I can't go back to that life. I have to make this new life work, no matter what. Out of desperation more than determination, she swung a small backpack onto her back containing all of her life's possessions. She secured the ponytail holding back her thick brown hair, took off her sunglasses, and cradled them in her right hand. Her slim body ungracefully dove off the side of the boat straight into the clear, sparkling water. She started swimming to shore.

Chester yelled from his boat. "Wait, Miss! Where are you going? There are rumors about that island. I never gave them any credence until I saw the place. That isn't the kind of place I want to drop anyone off. Please come back. I'll take you anywhere else you want to go."

Gina walked up onto shore dripping wet. She slid her glasses back on and turned around to wave at Chester. "Thank you again for bringing me to Riley's Paradise Island. I have it from here."

Gina thought she heard him say something about crazy women but couldn't be sure over the waves gently rushing onto the shore. She turned around and walked into the jungle along the largest path she could find leading away from the docks. *I need to dry out my bag soon. I only have two changes of clothing, my last forty dollars, and a hairbrush they gave me at the shelter.*

Tree limbs covered the path and plants were already growing upright in the middle of the walkway, showing that no one had cared for it in a while. *What have I gotten myself into? Maybe Chester was right. I should have gone back with him. If I had anywhere else to go, I would have.*

Despite the chaos, the jungle was full of life. Monkeys chattered as they swung through the trees. Birds sang as they flew through the canopy. Insects buzzed as they went about their business of pollinating the plentiful flowers lining her path. There was a beauty to the surrounding disorder that was breathtaking. She had seen nothing quite like it before in her life.

At one point, Gina caught her foot in a simple slipknot animal trap. *Odd that it would be right along a main walking path. Whoever set it must not know much about trapping.* She didn't know a ton, but it looked set way too big to catch any local wild game. Gina didn't think too much of it as she loosened the loop around her foot and reset the trap with a smaller loop as best as she could off the path.

A large tree with a structure attached like a treehouse had fallen across her path. She spotted a can of food lying on the ground and picked it up. She added it to her pack, not sure how she would get it open.

After several hours of circumventing obstacles, she came upon a large Mexican-style hacienda. It was brown with green trim and looked like they built it to blend in with the surrounding jungle. A large tree had fallen on the house and crumpled a part of the roof. *Looks like I found the owner's house. I hope they aren't mad that I'm late. It took me longer to navigate this island than I planned. I was supposed to be at work by nine a.m. today and it's already closer to noon.*

She took the comb out of her pack and brushed her hair before putting it back into the ponytail. She tried to smooth out her mostly dried clothing, took off her sunglasses, and stashed them in her pack. *I wish I had something nicer to wear for my first day of work. I probably look like something the tide brought in.*

She made her way to the main entrance. There were two metal lattice doors, one behind the other, that looked like they led into a courtyard of some type. They reminded her of the portcullis gates of a castle.

To the left of the door, there was a keypad. She tried activating it by touching it, making sure it turned on, but it didn't respond at all. *Great, it's not working. I wonder what else the storm damaged. Hopefully, the kitchen is still serviceable.*

Gina called out through the gate. "Hello! Is someone there? It's me, Gina. I'm here to start work as your chef." No one answered. Dread filled Gina's stomach. No one was waiting for her.

What if Chester was right? What if they have evacuated the island? Come to think of it, they would have had no way of alerting me if they left. As soon as I secured this job, I left home and didn't leave a forwarding number. What have I gotten myself into?

Gina opened her backpack and lay the contents out in the sun to dry. They already smelled musty from being in her pack for so long. She secured the forty dollars under a rock. A lot of good that would do her out in the middle of the jungle.

She made her way back through the forest until she came to the treehouse. *I found a can of food here. Maybe more supplies fell out when this tree crashed. Although, why someone would live in a treehouse when there is a giant house nearby, I can't guess.*

After searching for a few hours, she found a can opener and a knife. There was a metal net attached to the bottom of the treehouse, but she couldn't get it free and didn't know what she would do with it if she did. She was hoping to find more, but at least she could have a meal before she figured out what to do tomorrow.

Gina used the can opener to open the can of chicken noodle soup. She slurped it down cold from the can. *I'm still starving. It has to be close to dinner time by now.* What should I do for the night? Gina climbed through the window of the treehouse, lying on the ground. A monkey yelled at her as it scampered out the other window.

She stood up on one wall that was now a floor. It was slightly crumpled where it fell but was otherwise intact. A broken table lay in the corner of the room. *Well, I guess this is better than sleeping out in the open.*

Gina left to gather her things that were now dry. To her horror and dismay, the forty dollars was gone.

FREE Reads! Blundering Through Paradise

Their thirst for adventure has turned into a fight to survive...
Brothers Jackson and Nathan wanted to reconnect for the summer on their island home. What better way than trying to impress the women they are pining for by catching a crew of smugglers raiding their tropical paradise?

It seemed simple enough. Set traps and let the island do the rest. Unfortunately, unforeseen obstacles sprung up, and Jackson and Nathan find themselves fighting for their lives. Uncovering riddles.

Deciphering clues. As Nathan and Jackson blunder through their life-or-death adventure, they learn a little something about the greatest mystery of all... love.

Embark on adventure in this prequel novella featuring beloved characters from ***Puzzling Through Paradise Series***.

10 Prequel Scenes from the Loves Cats Series
Excerpt from Willa's Blooper Reel

Katrina sorted all the fresh flowers into piles around her living room. *This smells wonderful. I hope they keep this powerful scent for the shower tomorrow.* She sat down in the only open space left on the floor and looked around her.

She had twenty-three flower centerpieces to finish by tomorrow. They were going to meet at eight in the morning to set up the hall for her sister, Susan's bridal shower. *I wish I had an easier time at work today. I was hoping to be fresher before tackling this.*

I'm just swamped at work right now. We had a lot of new cats come in recently. Last week, one of my volunteers told me they got a new job, and she doesn't have the time to help anymore. Another told me today that they were moving. It looks like I will be recruiting new volunteers next week.

Katrina picked up one of the glass vases and groaned. *This is going to take me all night, but what choice do I have? I guess I will have to stay up as late as it takes to finish this project.* She turned on the television in the background and filled the bottom of the vases with glass beads.

Willa sat napping behind her on the couch while she fiddled around with the flowers. Katrina tried a few different arrangements until she got the perfect look. She fiddled around with tying a perfect bow from the coordinating ribbon and then snapped a picture to send to her sister.

Good. One arrangement done, twenty-two to go. At my current rate of one flower arrangement per every half hour, that's only eleven more hours to go. Katrina put her head in her hands. *What have I gotten myself into?*

Katrina got to work. At one point, Willa came over and sat on top of a pile of flowers. "No, no, Willa. Come on. You can't sit there. You'll smash them. Here, it's almost dinnertime. Why don't I get you some food?" Katrina got up and poured cat food into Willa's dish. Willa munched happily as Katrina went back to work.

Luckily, now that she got the design down, she pumped out eight more arrangements over the next two hours. Katrina was midway through the next one when she decided that she really needed a break. She stood up, stretched her legs, and made some tea.

When she got back into the living room, she sat back down in front of her partially finished arrangement. *I thought I already put a purple one in there.* She picked up a new purple one. *I guess I didn't. The flowers are already running together.*

Katrina had twelve arrangements complete when she noticed that there were half as many of the yellow flowers as the pink and purple ones. *Oh no. The florist must have miscounted. I don't have enough yellow. What can I do? Maybe if we use the ones with yellow flowers on every other table, it won't be a big deal that some have yellow and some don't.*

She tried out arranging a centerpiece with no yellow flowers and added extra baby's breath so that they still looked full and put it beside the completed arrangements that had yellow. *I like it. Instead of being overwhelmed with yellow, it gives more of a hint of yellow.* Convinced it solved the problem, Katrina continued on.

Around two in the morning, Katrina was down to her last two arrangements. She was growing cross-eyed and developed a weird aversion to pink, purple, and yellow flowers. She reached for a flower to her side, when she realized that there were none of the pink flowers left.

Katrina became suspicious and looked around. *It's one thing if the florist miscounted the yellow flowers, but I recounted the pink and purple ones only a few hours ago. The only one other living thing in the house was... Willa.*

Katrina turned around to see Willa innocently sitting on the couch behind her. Unfortunately, the thief made a mistake. Upon closer inspection, she saw a yellow flower petal in her fur. Exhausted, she sternly asked, "Willa, what have you been doing with my flowers?"

Willa continued to look on, completely innocent. Katrina pretended like she was back at work, making another flower arrangement, while carefully watching the remaining purple flowers.

Out of the corner of her eye, she watched Willa silently pad over to the flower pile. She picked a flower up in her jaws and traveled behind the couch to sneak it out of the room, unseen. Katrina stood up slowly to see where she was taking the flower.

Willa turned the corner into her bedroom and climbed under the bed. There she laid her latest acquisition on-top of a nest of flowers she made. Immediately, she rolled all over them, crumpling the new flower to match the other ruined flowers.

Katrina felt like she could cry. *I worked so hard on these arrangements all night. I'm so close to finishing. Where am I going to get more fresh flowers at this time of night?* She gently scolded Willa for taking things that weren't hers. Willa lowered her head and slunk further under the bed, knowing she was caught.

Katrina picked up the scattered pieces of flowers. *There's no salvaging these. I simply don't have time to go pick up new flowers tomorrow morning. These last two centerpieces were for the head table. I can't just set them up there with a few purple flowers and some leftover baby's breath flowers.*

Willa looked out under the bed and softly meowed. A cranky Katrina scowled. "Maybe I should put you in one of the centerpieces. At least then it would look full. Then Susan could bring her cat, Biscuit, to put in the second one. It would look perfectly full and balanced." The offhanded comment sparked an idea in Katrina's mind.

***

The next morning, Susan gushed over the flower arrangements. "I can't believe you finished these all yourself! They turned out beautiful and smell great too."

A bit about Miranda Herald

Typing by moonlight and powered by tea, I love reading and writing whenever I can fit it in. I find a good mind boggling puzzle or escape room exhilarating and was excited to include them in my latest works. I hope you enjoy my puzzling twist on romance and join my characters for many more adventures!

I love to hear from my readers and want you to join my community on Facebook, Tiktok, and Instagram. Check out my website to find all of my freebies, novels, and social links. You can find everything at my website **www.mirandaherald.com.**

Join my subscription community for pre-release books and exclusive exclusive content!

https://reamstories.com/page/ldxyuocbpf

9 7 9 8 9 8 7 2 5 1 5 1 5